A Love that Spans the Ages

—Emile N. Joseph—

A Love that Spans the Ages
Emile N. Joseph

📖Nightlight Books

Formatted by Proton Writing Consultants Pty Ltd
www.WritersMarke.com | info@WritersMarke.com
PO Box A2379 | Sydney South | NSW 1235 | Australia

ISBN-13: 978-0-9875530-9-6

Disclaimer
All characters appearing in this work are fictitious. Any
resemblance to real persons, living or dead, is purely
coincidental.

To Violet

My Lady,
My Life,
My Love.

CONTENTS

ACKNOWLEDGEMENTS

I thank you, Ramy Tadros, my friend, my mentor and my publisher, without whose inspiration, aid, encouragement and advice this work would never have seen the light of day.

I thank you, my mother Mary, my father Emile and my sister Susan, my aunts, uncles and cousins for all your love, support and care throughout my life, from childhood to adulthood.

I thank you, my friends: Luke, Philip and Peter, Christian, Gunnar, Priscilla, Peter H., Jonathon and Victoria.

I also thank you, my former headmaster Mr R. West, in whose school I learned not only the classics and the riches of English literature, but the eternal verities of the Christian faith.

I thank you, my father- and mother-in-law, and all my brothers- and sisters-in-law, for accepting and welcoming me into your family and allowing me to marry your dear daughter and sister.

I thank you and love you, my dear wife Violet, for loving me, supporting me, believing in me and showing me your constant devotion. You have made my life the prelude to Paradise. You have inspired me, changed me and made me a better man. You have also given me the blessed opportunity to be a father to two precious little children. I love you with all my heart.

Last but not least, I give thanks to Thee, my Lord Jesus Christ, who hast always been by my side as I was writing this novella, and who hast inspired me all the way through. To Thee be the glory forever and ever, and to the ages of all ages.

TRANSLATOR'S NOTES FOR THE TEXT
THE CONFESSIONS OF BROTHER BENEDICT

For simplicity, I have translated the date as 1414, since these events started in February of that year. However, by fifteenth century reckoning, the calendar year commenced on 25 March, the Feast of the Annunciation.

Although I have translated all of the text into Modern English, I have decided to preserve the pronouns *thou* and *thee* etc. in the speech of Sir Dominic and Rose because it captures the essence of their poetic speech at a level of intimacy which the simple pronoun *you* fails to bring across. I also wish to convey that Sir Dominic's speech was more poetic than usual, as was Rose's, when she was with him. I have used *you* everywhere else, whenever this poetic intimacy was not relevant.

Regarding the hours of the day, people living in mediaeval times did not divide the day into twenty-four hours as we do, and did not usually count the hours in minutes and seconds. Their day was divided according to the canonical hours (the monastic cycle of daily prayer), according to which the church bells rang. Matins corresponded to midnight, Lauds to 3 am, Prime was from 6 am to 9 am, Terce from 9 am to 12 pm, Sexte from 12 pm to 3 pm and None (from which we get the word "noon") was originally from 3 pm to 6 pm, but later covered the period from 12 pm to 6 pm. Vespers began at 6 pm and ended at 9 pm (Compline), which marked the end of the day, at which hour all towns had a curfew, after which only people with lanterns, guards and people of good reputation were allowed to travel in the streets.

A manor was all the land which a lord owned and which he allotted to tenants to work and live on (with rent). Some tenants, who were wealthy and in a high social position, held their own land, granted by the lord of the manor. An example of such a tenant is a yeoman, a privileged peasant with a free holding of fifty acres or more. The homes of peasant landholders were called messuages, which included a house and a parcel of land around it for gardening and keeping animals. The house in which the lord and his household dwelt was called a manor house.

A kirtle was like a long gown, and women wore them long, usually down to their ankles. A doublet was the vest that knights wore when dressed in civilian clothes, or under their armour.

~Part 1~

The Confessions of Brother Benedict

I

In the year of Our Lord 1414, I attended a banquet to celebrate the betrothal of Sir Dominic and of his beautiful bride-to-be, Rose. The festivities, held in Lord Godwin's sumptuous manor hall, were truly magnificent, and there were at least one hundred people present, including many knights, noblemen and women, ladies and dames, as well as Rose's father and mother.

Sir Dominic has always been more of a friend than a master, and that is why my sinful actions against him were all the more reprehensible. I regret bitterly what I did to him, even though he has forgiven me. Anyway, I have many years in this monastery to do penance for my wicked deeds.

Sir Dominic, at the time of his betrothal, was a handsome young man of twenty-one summers, who had just become a knight a few months before. He was six feet tall, of strong build, with a wide chest and broad, manly shoulders. He had an aquiline nose, blue eyes, long dark brown hair and a beard. He was a strong and courageous knight.

His betrothed, Rose, was of both English and French descent because her father, the yeoman Master Adam Thorne, married a wealthy French merchant's daughter residing in Cambridge, and owned a house and parcel of land of about fifty acres.

Rose was a superb specimen of a young woman: long, golden hair flowing down to the small of her back, crystalline blue eyes, rosy lips and a slender form. Sir Dominic was clearly in love with her, and found it difficult to take his eyes off her.

Sir Dominic and Rose were so clearly enraptured in each other's presence that even their words took flight. Sir Dominic always had a poetic manner of speaking, because he dedicated so much of his time to reading the great works of poetry ever since he was a child, and even composed ballads of his own. Poetry became like second nature to him, and now that he was in love, one could say that he spoke poetry as soon as he opened his mouth. As far as I know, no man spoke like this man, at least in my lifetime. Rose, elated by the same love, seemed to catch the poetic spirit, as if by contagion.

As an example of their speech, here are the words which Sir Dominic spoke to Rose during the banquet, before the entertainment commenced:

"My dearest damsel, 'tis a splendid day
This day we are betrothed, and yet I feel
That we have been for centuries like this.
O lovely Rose, how dear thou art to me!
How fortunate I am to be with thee!"

And this is how Rose replied:

"Oh no, my dear, 'tis I who ought to be
Called fortunate, for thou are great and noble
And damsels all would kill to take my place."

Sir Dominic, enthralled by the deepest passion, almost sang these words in response:

"I love thee, Rose, the fairest of thy race
I love thee for thy simple, trusting heart,
I love thee for thy virtue, modesty
And honesty, the beauty of thy soul,
As well as of thy form, thy radiant face.
I love thee for I chose thee first of all.
I chose thee for I love thee, I avow."

And Rose, blushing, replied:

"O Dominic, I know for certain now
With thee shall I be happy all my days."

I recorded these beautiful words, which I can somehow still remember, after one year, for they are as fresh to me as if they had been uttered yesterday.

And that is why my sinful deeds, against this beautiful, innocent couple and against God, were so grievous.

There was one significant person absent from the festivities that day, a certain Cassandra Cole of Kent. I knew her briefly a year prior to Sir Dominic's betrothal to Rose, because he courted Cassandra then. She had been a frequent visitor at Wright Hall, which was Lord Godwin's manor house, and knew the whole household, even me, a humble servant. I saw her as a fiery, red-haired beauty of remarkable intelligence, who had an impressive level of education for a young woman of our era.

She had left her parents in Kent, for a reason that she never fully disclosed, and lived in Cambridge town with her old uncle, an alchemist who taught her Latin, mathematics and the rudiments of his own craft.

Yes, she was a fine, enchanting young woman, but her period of courtship with Sir Dominic was not a happy one. After one or two months, they started to quarrel. It became apparent that Cassandra thought herself more intelligent than Sir Dominic, and even more than anyone in the manor with whom she discussed any matter, from classical medicine to Latin literature. Not only that, but I noticed that she always carried a small, hand-held mirror in her belt, and that she spent an inordinate amount of time gazing into it.

After a while, she would act as if she herself owned the manor, just because she was being courted by the lord's son. She became more and more arrogant with each passing day. Alas, everyone but I thought so at the time. For some unknown reason, which I still cannot comprehend, I found her attractive, enchanting, irresistible. I admired her intelligence and her beautiful, deep and seductively feminine voice. How foolish I was!

No matter how disagreeable and dominating Cassandra became, Sir Dominic still forgave her, time and time again, for such was his nature. His father, and all his household, pleaded with him to end the courtship, but he continued to give her one more chance, then another, then another.

Finally, she committed a misdeed which even Sir Dominic found it hard to forgive: she started to show evidence of an avid interest in the dark magical arts. When Sir Dominic, with tears welling up in his eyes, asked her why she was doing this, she replied that these arts were a natural extension of her studies in alchemy. Her uncle had died shortly before that day, and had bequeathed his fortune to her, and she told Sir Dominic with ardent enthusiasm about her new found science.

"Dear Dominic, if only you knew how much power and knowledge I am gaining thanks to the art of magic, you would dedicate yourself to it as well. You can have more knowledge and strength than all your peers! You can be the greatest and most powerful knight in all of Christendom! Consider it!"

Sir Dominic wept for her, and spoke to her sadly, in his unique, poetic way:

"My dear Cassandra, thou hast strayed, alas
On paths where I will never tread; farewell!
Thou hast betrayed me, and betrayed our faith,
Which … which … which …"

Sir Dominic, overcome with emotion, turned his head to hide his tears. Cassandra looked at him with contempt, then left Wright Hall, without so much as a courteous farewell to anyone.

II

Since Cassandra stormed out of Lord Godwin's manor house that day, no one had seen or heard from her. No one even knew whether she still resided in Cambridgeshire—until the day after the banquet during which the betrothal was announced.

I had completed my domestic duties for the day, and I was making my way into town to have a pint of ale at the tavern, as was my custom, when I saw her. Yes, it was she, Cassandra Cole of Kent, with her fiery red hair and her intense green eyes.

"Good evening to you!" I greeted her politely with a bow. "Tell me, are you by any chance Mistress Cassandra of Kent? Your face is familiar, but I can never be too sure."

"Yes, old fellow, it is I, Cassandra. But my name is Cassandra Caligo."

"Caligo? I remember it as Cole, if I am not mistaken."

"It was Cole, now it is Caligo. I hate my father and his name. But that is of no concern to you, ... I beg your pardon, I am afraid I cannot remember your name."

"My name is Tristan Miller," I replied, giving her the name that I used to have in the world before I took my vows and became a monk.

"Yes, Tristan Miller! I remember you well now. You were one of the brightest servants in the household of... of someone who claimed to love me."

"I thank you for the flattery, madam," I started, before she ushered me into an isolated alleyway.

"Sorry, but we must be discreet. I do not want anyone to see me around here. I am not very popular, you know."

"Oh yes, of course," I continued, unperturbed. "As I was saying, you flatter me, but I must say, on Sir Dominic's behalf …"

Cassandra seemed irritated.

"Do not utter that man's name in my presence! You know as well as I that he spurned me for no justifiable reason!"

"But, but—" I stammered.

"Never mind. Now that you have mentioned his name, what news do you have of him? Does he languish over the memory of me, regretting what he cast out?"

"No, I am sorry to say, but—"

And starting with these words, I made the first grave error.

"—but as a matter of fact, he is now betrothed to another."

"Really?" she replied, her lower lip quivering with barely contained rage. "Tell me, is she fair?"

I was about to sing the praises of Rose Thorne but stopped myself when I noticed that she probably did not share my enthusiasm about her rival's betrothal.

"Yes, I cannot lie, she is indeed fair—but not as fair as you."

I actually meant that because I considered Cassandra to be extremely beautiful.

"Hmmm, we shall see. What is her name?"

I hesitated. Should I tell her? Why did she desire to know her rival's name?

"Well?" she asked, impatiently.

"With all due respect, madam, why do you need to know her name?"

"I have my reasons."

"Rose, her name is Rose," I stammered, wondering whether I had just committed another very grave error.

"Rose … Rose …" she murmured to herself. "Listen, Tristan, if you are free for a moment, I should like you to come with me."

I gulped. Go with her? Where? For what purpose?

My first reaction as a dutiful servant and a loyal friend to Sir Dominic was to refuse. But she gazed at me with her seductive green eyes, smiled at me and touched my shoulder, and so I consented, to my great shame.

Cassandra rubbed her hands with glee.

"Very well, follow me."

"Yes, madam," I replied, as obediently as a lamb.

"And I pray you, call me by my name, Cassandra!"

"Very well, m … Cassandra."

She smiled, and led me through the isolated alleyway, and into another alleyway, where no one would notice us, and she kissed me. Not on the cheek, like friends or cousins, but on the lips. From that moment on, I was spellbound.

III

After that kiss, I was ready to follow Cassandra like a lamb to the slaughter. My conscience was struggling to convince me to flee for my life, but my legs were paralysed, or rather no longer in my control, but following Cassandra wherever she led me.

She led me to an old, run-down house at the end of a dark alley. Since it was still winter, it was dark by now, at the hour of vespers. She took out a key from a pocket under her kirtle, opened the front door, and beckoned me in. Foolishly, I entered. She closed the door behind me and locked it from the inside. Then she entered the kitchen, which was filthy, crawling with cockroaches and other vermin, and tapped her foot on a medium-sized square, which was of a different colour from the rest of the floor. The square turned on itself and opened, revealing an underground passageway. I followed her downstairs until we reached a long corridor lined with mirrors of all shapes and sizes. Cassandra, holding an oil lamp, led me through the corridor, and as I walked behind her like a puppy after his mistress, I looked at the mirrors, which were all as tall as we were, and which all showed us very flattering reflections of ourselves. In my eyes, Cassandra was already physically perfect, but I appeared far more muscular and robust than I really was.

We then entered a spacious chamber and Cassandra bid me be seated on a stool near a large table, which was placed in front of an enormous mirror. She sat on a red cushion atop a large wooden chair between the table and the mirror. I cast a quick glance around the chamber and noticed a great many bookshelves full of old and dusty books. I was burning with curiosity to peruse some of these books, but then Cassandra started to speak. I turned to her and noticed that her eyes were closed and that she was chanting these words in Latin:

"Speculum meum carum in muro
Dic mihi vero, te adjuro
Qualis virgo est ista Rosa?
Monstra mihi, estne formosa?"

Although my knowledge of Latin was by no means as good as Cassandra's, I knew enough to understand the rudiments. This is what she said, in layman's words: "My dear mirror on the wall / Tell me truly, I adjure you / What kind of maiden is this Rose / Show me, is she fair?"

The mirror then did an astounding thing. Firstly, it crackled, then emitted some odd sounds, like the screeching of an owl, then a bright light flashed, nearly blinding me. Finally, there in the mirror before me appeared the image of Rose Thorne, Sir Dominic's beloved, as accurate a portrait as the best artist in all of Christendom could have painted it. I stared at the likeness in awe and wonder, but Cassandra just laughed when she saw me staring with my mouth wide open.

"Golden hair, blue eyes, a fair complexion …" she mused, studying the image, "Aye, Sir Dominic has found a true delight!"

The cynicism in her voice was palpable.

"May I ask a question?" I stammered nervously.

"Sure," she said in an affable tone, which relieved me.

"When we met earlier, you were sorely vexed when I mentioned Sir Dominic's name, yet you have mentioned it now, and you have evidently gone to great trouble to find out how his betrothed looks. My question is: Why are you still thinking about Sir Dominic and his betrothed if you hate him so much? And why do you hate him so much?"

"Those are two questions! I shall answer the second one first, but really, there is only one answer for both. I hate him for he is a proud Christian, and, for no justifiable reason, he refused me, dismissed me disgracefully, merely because of my interest in the magical arts. I never betrayed him, I never lay with another man. I was merely thirsty for knowledge, and I was starting to see that the *occulta*, the hidden things, were teaching me more than the Christian faith. And he rejected me for that! Furthermore, he never allowed me to explain the merit of my studies. He was probably frightened by intelligent, powerful women. That is why he prefers to marry this simple, innocent, ignorant child, because she will always submit to him, and allow him to dominate her. Does this answer satisfy you?"

Her voice, normally seductive, sounded bitter. She noticed that her rant disturbed me, and said soothingly, "Never mind. This should not concern you. I know that Sir Dominic and Rose are your friends. I shall never interfere in that."

With those words, she kissed me again, and then led me to her bedchamber, which was also lined with mirrors. Her bed smelt of aromatic spices and perfumes from the Orient. What we did then shall forever remain a frightful stain on my conscience, and the sin for which I cry day and night for forgiveness and mercy.

By the grace of God, I managed to leave Cassandra's home and return to Wright Hall before the curfew. I entered by the servants' entrance, and no one asked me where I had gone and why. There was always an atmosphere of trust and mutual respect at Wright Hall, and that made me feel all the worse for abusing it.

IV

The next morning, Sir Dominic was the first to notice that I was troubled, and came to talk to me.

"My friend, you seem quite pale and ill today. Now tell me, did you drink too much last night?"

"No, sir," I replied. "I am not ill, but … I am concerned about a friend of mine."

It was so hard to lie to Sir Dominic; it grieved my heart because he always trusted my word and never doubted me. It was inconceivable that his loyal servant and friend would lie to him. I tried to make my words as truthful as possible, but there was still deceit, as I was purposefully concealing the true meaning of my words.

"And can you tell me something of this trouble?"

"No, I am afraid not, sir, although I would really like to tell you."

That part was true, so it was easier to say.

"No, let it be," said Sir Dominic. "You must not e'er betray / The confidence of one who trusts in you."

How those words stung me by their unintentional irony! That is exactly what I was doing! I could only nod and say, "Quite right, sir."

Sir Dominic was silent for a while before he invited me to join him on horseback.

"Where are you going, sir?" I asked.

"I go to see my lovely Rose again.

I need to see her beauty every day

As flowers need the sunlight and the rain.

So would you like to come with me today?"

"Certainly, sir! It would be my pleasure."

Sir Dominic led me on horseback to his betrothed damsel's home, which was a pretty little cottage with a garden and a field around it. I watched as Sir Dominic dismounted, stood under the window of Rose's bedchamber and called out to her with a song in his voice. She opened the window without delay and greeted him warmly and excitedly. She urged her beloved to wait a moment while she prepared to go out. She closed the window and the curtain and after a brief delay, she came out to meet Sir Dominic who was waiting patiently for her. She ran into Sir Dominic's arms to embrace him, full of joyful laughter. She then noticed me and curtsied respectfully, and I bowed in response. Rose's nurse appeared at the door as well, and asked the young couple not to stay out too long. Sir Dominic gave his word, and we all set off.

We left the horses tied up outside Rose's house and walked for an hour through the streets of Cambridge and along the banks of the River Cam, Sir Dominic and Rose walking hand in hand, and I walking a few feet behind them, so as not to disrupt their intimate dialogue.

After their stroll, and after Rose returned home, Sir Dominic turned to me with a smile and said,

"Now is she not the most delightful maiden?

Our nuptials, be they soon, seem far away.

For Rose, I would do anything at all

From now and till the end of this our age."

With those words, he took his leave, telling me that he had important affairs to which he had to attend. And I, the fool that I was, made my way towards my impending doom.

After I attended to all my duties, and asked for permission for leave, I sped as quickly and as surreptitiously as possible towards Cassandra's house, and knocked six times on the door, to let her know that it was I. She let me in, looked out cautiously, and locked the door behind me. We sat down at her table upstairs to eat some meat—I had no idea who provided it. While we ate, she asked me many questions about Sir Dominic and Rose, and I answered them all honestly, even questions about where Rose dwelt and where she had gone with Sir Dominic that day. I curse myself for answering her about confidential information, especially after Sir Dominic so graciously respected her privacy.

Strangely, she did not admit me to her basement that day. She explained that she was immersed in study at the time, but she promised to show me the fruits of her labour very soon. I was extremely curious, but she only laughed and said, "You will see it soon enough. Come by in about four days."

"Four days! I was hoping to see you again tomorrow! Cassandra ... I am ... I must confess that ... I am enamoured of you."

Cassandra tilted her head back and laughed.

"You are in love with me? How sweet!"

Then she kissed me and said, "You please me immensely, Tristan. I am certain that our love, our courtly love, will last a very long time. I am your lady, and you are my valiant knight. If you continue to work faithfully with me, I shall continue to bestow on you my ... favours."

She winked and said farewell. We kissed again, more passionately than ever before. Then I bowed and took my leave, burning with lust and shame at the same time.

At vespers, in the evening of the following day, since I was not going to see Cassandra, I went to the tavern for my usual pint of ale. My usual drinking companions were all there, including Ludovic the librarian, Philibert the philosopher, Conrad the clerk and Gregory the groom. Ludovic was the first to notice my presence as I entered.

"Hey Tristan!" he shouted. "Where have you been, my friend?"

"Yes," piped in Philibert. "We have not seen you these last few nights."

"Have you been ill?" asked Gregory.

"No," I answered, "Everything is fine. I have just been occupied."

"Occupied?" asked Ludovic. "Come on! Don't talk to us about being occupied! When you have to deal with hundreds of manuscripts and archives like me, then come and talk to me about being occupied!"

19

"Yes, you work too hard unnecessarily," added Philibert. "Everyone knows that Lord Godwin is very lenient on his servants. He is no hard taskmaster, by any means."

"Come, take a seat here!" said Ludovic, beckoning me to an empty chair next to him at the old wooden table. He then called out to the tavern keeper. "Master Thomas! A pint of ale for my good man Tristan! It's on me!"

The tavern keeper poured a goblet of the amber liquid and served it to me.

"Let's drink to His Majesty the King!" shouted Gregory.

We all drank to His Majesty, and then to Lord Godwin, and also to Sir Dominic and Rose Thorne. After our toasts were done, and the men were merrier, Ludovic drew next to me and said, in a quiet voice, "So Tristan, tell me the truth. Why have you been avoiding us? Have you been seeing a wench in secret? You can tell me."

I was astonished at Ludovic's powers of perception. I could not help but flinch.

"Aha! So there is a wench! Come on! Who is she? Spill it out!"

"She is no one special. Just your ordinary lass, a peasant's daughter whom I met at the markets one day. I doubt that there is any future in this dalliance. But Ludovic, to be frank, I would rather not talk about her at present. She is a discreet young woman, quite shy. She prefers to remain concealed."

I was surprising myself how cleverly I was mixing truth and lies to make it all sound convincing and not altogether false.

"This makes me all the more curious to know more!" said Ludovic. "Tell me at least her name!"

"Very well," I said, "draw closer."

I leaned over and whispered a false name into his ear. There was no way that I would ever have exposed Cassandra to anyone.

"Catherine?" repeated Ludovic. "What a lovely name! That name means 'pure', you know. Thank you for confiding in me."

"You're welcome", I answered, ashamed of myself for lying to my friend, but I had no choice.

"Well, three cheers for you, then!" said Ludovic merrily, raising his goblet and drinking to my health. We then drank in silence for a few minutes, listening to the others conversing in slurred voices.

Suddenly I overheard Conrad the clerk talking to Philibert the philosopher about a subject which interested me greatly.

"I hear that she's returned," said Conrad.

"Who?" asked Philibert. "You mean ... the witch?"

"Precisely," answered Conrad. "But keep your voice down."

It was no use lowering their voice, I could hear them as clearly as if they had been shouting in my ear.

"What business does she have coming to Cambridge?" asked Conrad, indignantly.

"I thought she left Cambridgeshire altogether," said Philibert, "after what she did to Sir Dominic and his household."

"Excuse me," I interjected, "I couldn't help overhearing. I am from Sir Dominic's household. Are you referring to——?"

"Precisely!" said Conrad. "We're talking about that witch! My friend Roderick the Reeve told me that he saw her frequenting these parts of town. How dare she!"

"She's bold, I have to say!" said Philibert. "If anyone catches her, it's the stake for her!"

"Yes," said Ludovic, joining in. "Everyone knows that Sir Dominic broke off his courtship with her because of her witchcraft."

"Yes, I know that she studies the magical arts with avid interest," I said. "Her late uncle was an alchemist, and he educated her. She is quite an intelligent young woman."

"She may be an intelligent young woman," scoffed Ludovic. "She may be gifted with extraordinary intelligence, but she has such an inflated opinion of herself! She thinks she is better than anyone else! What is she doing around here anyway? If we are not good enough for her, why is she loitering around here and not living in Italy, where the people are more cultured and refined?"

"I think she's up to no good, that's what I think!" said Conrad. "If any one of you sees her, tell me. I can tell Roderick to arrange for a band of soldiers to arrest her!"

"Here! Here!" said all of the men who were still sober. The others just belched and burped.

Deep down, I was burning with anger and confusion. I was in love with Cassandra, and here were my friends judging her so harshly and thirsting for her execution! They were my friends, yes, but they were being a bit too harsh on poor Cassandra, I thought. So what if she was proud! So what if she was interested in the magical arts! Was she hurting anyone? Who were they to judge? That was a matter between Cassandra and her Maker.

Ludovic turned to me and said, "I would rather be a lonely monk in a cloister than involved in any way with a witch like Cassandra!"

"I hear you," I said, my soul in turmoil.

Over the next three evenings, my time spent at the tavern was more or less in the same vein as that first one since my return. I listened out for more tidings concerning Cassandra, but nothing new was said. I was relieved that no one from the tavern knew where Cassandra resided, no one had ever seen her by day, and no one even mentioned her name. They just referred to her as "the witch", "the sorceress" or other less complimentary titles. And more to the point, no one had the shadow of a suspicion that I was involved with her in any way, not even Ludovic, who was convinced that I was in love with a pure maiden called Catherine. Nevertheless, I resolved to take precautions and conceal myself more thoroughly when going to meet her.

V

Four days finally passed, and after completing my domestic duties, I told the other servants that I was going to drink a pint at the tavern. They all trusted me, and no one even thought of verifying my destination. Now in retrospect, I wish that they had. I may have been publicly humiliated, and even expelled from Wright Hall, but that would have been far better, in my opinion, than being covered in the foul stench of mortal sin.

When I reached Cassandra's house and knocked on the door, I found to my surprise that it opened by itself. I said to myself that Cassandra ought not to be so careless, because there were people who wanted her dead. The house was dark and empty. Where was Cassandra? Had she forgotten that I was coming? No, she was probably waiting for me to go down to the secret underground chamber. I entered the house, took an oil lamp from the kitchen table, and lit it. I then saw a small note scrawled in black ink on an old rag, which said, "I am waiting for you." I locked the main door and crept slowly and quietly towards the secret square, killing two or three cockroaches in the process; I tapped on the square, and entered the underground passageway. I passed through the corridor of mirrors, looking at my flattering reflection as I went through. As I approached the secret underground chamber, I could hear Cassandra's voice, but she was not speaking in English. I stopped, extinguished the light of the oil lamp and drew closer to the door, as quietly as possible. I wanted to listen to what she was saying without her knowing.

With my ear to the door, I listened to her speak to someone in Latin. It was probably her mirror. At first, she was murmuring and humming, so I could not make out what she was saying. Then she raised her voice and almost shouted. From what I could understand, this is what she was saying: *"I will not stand by and let my enemy, the man who spurned me, enjoy that damsel! By Lucifer, I shall destroy his pleasure! I shall pluck that sweet fruit from his garden! If Dominic will not have me, he shall have no one!"*

If this did not disturb me enough, what followed made my blood chill and my skin crawl. I heard a demonic voice, which sounded like a wild boar grunting and squealing while wallowing in bubbling sewage. I could not make out the words, but it was horrifying enough even if I did not know what the words meant.

I turned quickly to flee. I had seen and done enough. My friends were right: I should never have been involved with this woman! I could not stay anymore. Now I realised why Cassandra had changed her surname to Caligo: Caligo is Latin for darkness. I wanted to kick myself for not realising that before. This red-haired woman, who had seduced me and with whom I was so infatuated, was tampering with the powers of darkness.

As I was trying to flee, I unfortunately made a noise. The demonic voice ceased. There was a deathly pause, then Cassandra called out, "Tristan, is that you?"

I could not answer, I was so paralysed with fear.

"Tristan, come in here. I am alone."

I stood rooted to the spot. Cassandra ran up to the door and opened it from the other side.

"Tristan! You disappoint me! What were you doing eavesdropping? What did you hear?"

"Not much, since I only arrived now. And what I could hear, I could not understand."

This half-truth relieved her. And it was a good thing that she did not know how much Latin I could actually understand.

"Come with me! Come with me! I will show you something."

She led me like an excited school pupil impatient to show her schoolmaster the work that she had done. She led me into the chamber with the large mirror and told me to stand back and watch. I complied, terrified out of my wits, but curious nonetheless.

She stood in front of the mirror with her back to me and shouted, *"APPAREAT ROSA!"*

Instantly, after all the unearthly sounds and light effects, there appeared in the mirror the portrait of Rose Thorne, as it did before.

"Wait and see!" said Cassandra, unable to contain her excitement. Then she shouted, *"MUTER IN IMAGINEM SPECULI!"*

I beheld the spectacle of smoke and preternatural noises, and then, to my astonishment, Rose turned around and smiled at me! Well, it was not really Rose, of course, it was Cassandra, but the resemblance was perfect.

"Well, what do you say?" said Cassandra disguised as Rose. "Is this not an incredible accomplishment?"

I gaped in even more astonishment than when I saw her, because even her voice was now the voice of Rose, with all its inflections and even its hint of a French accent.

"How ... How ... did you do that?" I stammered, incredulous.

"My dear Tristan, can you see now how wonderful and spectacular the magical arts are? And Sir Dominic so quickly dismissed them as an affront to his faith! He knows not the delights and the power that could be at his fingertips! But you, Tristan, you can see merit in my magic, can you not? Will you join me in my magnificent pursuits? You can leave Wright Hall once and for all, and be your own man! You need no longer serve Sir Dominic or Lord Godwin or anyone. You can master the magical arts and become master of your own destiny! Will you join me?"

As she held out her hand to me, and pleaded to me in that seductive voice, I confess that I found her invitation tempting. However, I was still disturbed by what I had heard earlier, and by the fact that Cassandra was saying all of this in her disguise as Rose.

"I am sorry to ask you this, Cassandra, but could you say all that again as yourself, and not as Rose?"

Cassandra was irritated, but reluctantly complied with my request.

"*REVERTAR IN ME IPSAM!*" she exclaimed, and became herself again. She repeated her invitation to collaborate with her in the power and the glory of the magical arts. I hesitated. Too much was at stake here, as you realise.

"You hesitate?" asked Cassandra incredulously. "Need I convince you further? Behold the power of sorcery! *APPAREAT TRISTANUS!*"

These last words in Latin were spoken to her mirror, which made my image appear as if I had been looking into it, except that I was two feet away, standing behind Cassandra.

"*MUTER IN IMAGINEM SPECULI!*"

After all the preternatural effects, I saw before me a person who resembled me in every way. This was quite disconcerting, and did nothing to convince me of the attraction of the dark arts.

"I can appear as anyone I like!" boasted Cassandra, in my voice and accent. "Is it not wonderful?"

Hearing and seeing myself as another person really disturbed me. Naturally, Cassandra believed that she impressed me. But this appearance as me was a blessing in disguise, if you permit my play on words. It distanced me from Cassandra's fiery beauty, which seduced me in the first place, and allowed me to see myself as if I had accepted her invitation and collaborated with her in the dark arts. For although the person before me resembled me in voice and appearance, there was something missing. The Tristan before me appeared cold and soulless.

"REVERTAR IN ME IPSAM!" shouted Cassandra, as she reverted to her own form. She seemed irritated that I was not responding to her as quickly or following her as adoringly as I had done about a week ago.

"Now behold my most magnificent transformation! *APPAREAT MILES DOMINICUS!"*

After his image appeared in the mirror, she shouted again, *"MUTER IN IMAGINEM SPECULI!"*

After the unearthly sounds and the flash of light, there appeared before me the exact likeness of Sir Dominic Wright. I gasped, even though I expected the transformation. I almost bowed, but I stopped myself.

Cassandra laughed, but it sounded just like Sir Dominic.

"Bow to me, if you please! For I am your master, Sir Dominic!"

Although "he" resembled Sir Dominic perfectly in appearance, voice and timbre, "Pseudo-Dominic", this false Sir Dominic, was disturbingly unnatural in some way, like my image and Rose's before that. It was as if someone had painted his portrait, and the portrait came to life and started walking and talking, but without a soul.

Then I was struck with a terrible thought.

"Excuse me, Cassandra, what are you planning to do with this new power? I fear that you might use this 'gift' of yours for ill rather than for good."

"That, my friend, is none of your concern!"

"But Cassandra—"

"Call me Sir Dominic! Bow to me!"

"But you are not Sir Dominic!"

"Very well!" she retorted, clearly irritated. "You are not playing my game anymore! *REVERTAR IN ME IPSAM!*"

After she changed back to herself, she turned her back and took something out of a small compartment near her bookshelf. She threw the object in my direction, and because of my surprise, I failed to catch it. I bent down to pick up the small bag.

"It is a bag of money!" I exclaimed, opening it to see how much it contained. It was about 6 pence, which was the daily wage of a skilled labourer—a considerable amount.

"This is what I owe you for your trouble," she said coldly. "Do not say that I am unfair."

"What trouble? Cassandra, it was a pleasure to be with you."

"Do not lie! It is not becoming of you."

I was shocked. Here was Cassandra dismissing me, after all the intimate moments that we shared.

"So you no longer require my assistance or my company?"

"No," she replied coldly. "If you do not join me, you might as well oppose me."

"But Cassandra—"

"Call me madam, knave!"

"I am no knave! I am Tristan Miller, servant to Lord Godwin and to his son, Sir Dominic Wright, and to his daughters …"

"You are no one! You have no significance. As you have seen, I can produce your exact likeness without any effort."

"But you have not produced my soul, my spirit, my inner essence!"

"What is the soul? What is the spirit? It is a figment of the imagination, invented by superstitious Christians to frighten good and innocent people and keep them subjugated."

"Madam, I implore you not to do anything to harm Sir Dominic or Rose or anyone of their households. Remember your promise not to interfere in my friendship with them."

"I shall indeed not interfere in your paltry friendship with them, whatever that is worth!" She laughed, pointing to the money bag. But what I do with them is frankly not your concern!"

I started to become angry now. It was evident that Cassandra had used me to obtain all manner of news and information about Rose in order to destroy her. She had exhausted my supply now, so she was discarding me like refuse.

I stared at her in anger, barely able to contain myself. It was not in my nature to express my rage openly, but my eyes must have communicated my deep hurt.

"You may leave now, knave."

I turned on my heels and left, without so much as a bow or a farewell. But I did not reach the corridor of mirrors before she called me back.

"O Tristan!"

"Yes?" I answered hastily, pleased that she used my name again.

"If you so much as whisper a word of this to anyone, I shall make sure that everyone knows what you did with me and how you betrayed your master and his betrothed. You shall then be cast out in disgrace. Then I shall hunt you down and kill you personally. Is that clear?"

"Yes, madam."

"Good. You may now leave!"

"I thank you humbly, madam," I said with a bow. "Godspeed."

Cassandra emitted a serpentine hiss and slammed the door in my face. Slowly and sadly, I walked out of Cassandra's house for the last time. Even the magic mirrors in the corridor no longer gave me a flattering reflection, but instead showed the image of a withered and pathetic figure.

VI

Thanks be to God! The next morning, after I arose from my bed, I felt an enormous feeling of calm and relief, as if a great weight had been removed from my soul. But almost immediately after that, I started to worry again, because I knew that Cassandra desired to destroy Rose any way she could, or if not that, to destroy all hopes of her joining in holy matrimony to Sir Dominic. When Rose was with Sir Dominic or at home, she was safe, but if Cassandra ever found her alone … I was determined never to let that happen.

When Sir Dominic asked me to accompany him at noon that day, I readily acquiesced. It was good to be with Sir Dominic. I felt peace and comfort with him. And I enjoyed listening to him speak.

When we reached Rose's house, Sir Dominic dismounted and signalled to me to wait. He went and stood under her window and called out to her, as he was wont to do.

"O Rose, beloved Rose, come out, behold!

For early have I come to thee today!"

Sir Dominic waited. No answer. He waited a little longer before calling out again,

"Pray tell, is my dear Rose too ill to come

And greet her bridegroom waiting down below?"

Rose's window opened, but to our surprise, her nurse appeared to give us the unpleasant news: "Sir, Mistress Rose is not disposed to go out at this hour. She is not well. It appears that she ate some bad fruit at breakfast and has suffered a little indigestion. She asks you kindly to return at a later hour, perhaps at sunset."

"I thank you for your kind response, dear nurse.

I beg you tell my Rose I shall return

At some more fitting hour, at her request.

I pray that she recover soon today,

And tell her that I burn in love for her."

The nurse smiled and nodded and closed the window. Sir Dominic, downcast, mounted his horse again. I mounted my horse too and started to ride alongside him.

"So Tristan, it was not to be right now.

I shall return for her in two more hours

Perhaps she will be well enough to stroll,

As we are wont each day, albeit early."

With that, Sir Dominic rode off to see to some affairs.

I started to ride into town after him, but stopped. I excused myself, pretending to have some pressing domestic duties (which was true!). I had a very bad feeling about all of this.

As I made my way back to Rose's house, my worst fears were confirmed. I saw Rose's nurse wandering around the back of the house. I dismounted a little way off, so that the nurse might not see me, and tied my horse to a post. I then crept quietly and hid behind the wall of the house to spy on the nurse. She went behind a shrub, holding a small familiar mirror in her hand. Then after a few moments, someone else emerged from the shrub. It was Sir Dominic! Only I knew that it could not have been Sir Dominic, because I had seen him depart. It was Cassandra in disguise!

This false Sir Dominic, or Pseudo-Dominic if you will, stood under Rose's window, ready to call to her, when she opened it, leaned on the window-sill with her elbow and sighed.

"O dearest Dominic, forgive my folly.

How sad thou must have been when I came not

At noon to greet thee and to pass the time

In colloquy and walking hand in hand."

My first reaction was to shout out to Rose to warn her that this was not Sir Dominic, but I knew that such an action would have been sheer folly. In Rose's mind, it was inconceivable that someone who looked like Sir Dominic, and spoke with his voice, was not actually Sir Dominic. If any others had been in the house at that time, they would have come out and seen Sir Dominic and Rose and would hardly have believed me. Cassandra in disguise could have easily denounced me before them, and it would have been Sir Dominic's word against mine, to all appearances. No, it was not the time to expose her. I had to bide my time and find another opportunity.

Meanwhile, Pseudo-Dominic smiled and called out, "Rose, my Rose!"

"O Dominic," she replied, "can I in truth suppose

That it is truly thou who standest here?"

"No!" I muttered to myself from my hiding place. "It is not! Rose, beware!" What use was it? She could not hear me anyway. I pondered my strategy carefully. Should I go and find Sir Dominic? No, in that time, Cassandra would have abducted Rose, and then who knew what might happen? No, it was up to me to act. I betrayed my master and his betrothed before; now I had to betray Cassandra and rescue Rose.

"Aye, 'tis I, my sweet damsel. Come out hither, I await thee eagerly."

Rose's brow furrowed. She looked out of the window and saw her betrothed smiling at her. It was his face, his voice and his tone, but something was not right. She spoke no words, but I could almost hear her thoughts from the expression on her face. Sir Dominic spoke differently, of course, and she seemed to notice it. But then she smiled again, told Pseudo-Dominic to wait and hurried out the door without a word to anyone, except to shout, "Sir Dominic is here!" Within the blink of an eye, she was running out the door and into Sir Dominic's embrace. Her mother, Madam Eveline, waved to them from the door and then went back in. Pseudo-Dominic walked with Rose until they made a little distance from her home, and then he accelerated his pace a little as they walked towards the nearest woodland. Rose looked at Sir Dominic but seemed troubled.

I had to think fast. There had to be a way for me to lead Sir Dominic, Rose's parents or anyone to the place where Pseudo-Dominic was leading Rose. I had no idea what to do, but plucking up my courage, I followed the couple from a distance.

It was then that a small accident turned out to be a blessing in disguise: I stepped in some manure. I raised my foot in disgust to see the result of my clumsiness, but stepped on a twig when I put my foot down again. Pseudo-Dominic and Rose turned around quickly.

"O Tristan, it is you!' exclaimed Rose, almost with a sigh of relief.

Pseudo-Dominic seemed intent to murder me with his eyes, but remembered the disguise and simulated kindness. He was forced to reiterate Rose's invitation, because that was what the real Sir Dominic would have done. I said yes, and followed them at a short distance, within earshot. Then the couple walked silently hand in hand. Rose seemed disturbed by what she thought was Sir Dominic's strange behaviour and looked back at me with pleading eyes, seeking an explanation. Finally, she found the courage and the words, turned to Pseudo-Dominic and said,

"My dearest knight, 'tis good that we are now

Together in each other's company

But wherefore art thou sullen and so quiet?

Have I so vexed thee that thou art so cold

Towards me? Pray, forgive me, I was ill."

"I know," replied Pseudo-Dominic coldly. "Too ill even to see me?"

They continued their walk in silence. Pseudo-Dominic held her hand tightly and she was wincing and trying to release her hand from the vice-like grip. Suddenly, she tore herself from his grip with a surprising burst of strength, looked at him angrily and then started to cry. Pseudo-Dominic looked at her coldly, then slapped her squarely on the cheek. Rose screamed, more in shock and distress than in pain, and fell to the ground. She started to sob uncontrollably. Pseudo-Dominic looked around, then picked Rose up and hauled her over his shoulder like a bag of corn, and started to run through the woods.

Thinking on my feet, I looked for something to throw at Pseudo-Dominic. I looked on my person, and found the money bag which Cassandra had given me the day before. Savouring the irony, I hurled the bag with all my might at Pseudo-Dominic's head, careful not to strike Rose. Thanks be to God, I hit my target! Pseudo-Dominic howled in pain, dropped Rose onto the ground (making her scream) and turned around, holding the back of his head, which was bleeding. Rose, sobbing, looked up at Pseudo-Dominic and cried,

"O why hast thou so dealt with me today?

What horrid deed of mine deserved all this?"

"Rose, my lady," I interjected, "this is not your beloved Sir Dominic. He would never treat you in such an abject manner. This is an impostor. Mistress Cassandra, reveal yourself!"

"Mistress Cassandra?" Rose repeated, astonished and confused.

Pseudo-Dominic, laughed mockingly.

"Rose," said Pseudo-Dominic, "if you believe this liar, you are a simple-minded fool! This knave pretends to be my servant but secretly carouses with immoral women and drunkards. Believe not a word that he says!"

Rose looked at this man who appeared to be her betrothed, but was using words in ways that Sir Dominic would never have used them. She could never recall a time when Sir Dominic ever degraded anyone or worse still, insulted her. He would never, for as long as she knew him, reveal secrets and make scandalous reports about his friends. She furrowed her brow and pierced Pseudo-Dominic with her scrutinising gaze. Then she said,

"Although I know not how it could be done
I sense that Tristan must be speaking truth.
You look like him and speak like him, I see
But you are not Sir Dominic at all."

With these words, Pseudo-Dominic flew into a rage and drew his sword. I drew my short sword as well, and we started to duel, as Rose watched, sobbing and distressed beyond compare. Unable to bear the spectacle of the duel between one who appeared to be her beloved Sir Dominic and his loyal servant and friend, she swooned.

Unfortunately, Pseudo-Dominic took advantage of my momentary concern for Rose as she swooned, to strike my side. I fell to the ground, holding my bleeding side, and expecting to die.

VII

As I lay on the ground in pain, holding my side and feeling my life draining out of my body, I heard hooves and a familiar voice. It was the real sir Dominic at last, dressed in his knight's armour, followed by his squire Peter and Master Adam, Rose's father. Pseudo-Dominic, seeing the real Sir Dominic, shouted and ran away as fast as "he" could. As Pseudo-Dominic ran away, "his" form changed gradually, the knight's civilian attire transforming into a long woman's kirtle, the boots turning into slippers, and the hair becoming fiery red. Perplexed as to the reason for Cassandra's involuntary transformation, I looked at Sir Dominic, who had dismounted and run to Rose's side. He was praying and tears were streaming down his cheeks when he saw her in that sorry state. I could barely think at that time, but now I am certain that Sir Dominic's prayers divested Cassandra of her magical disguise.

Master Adam came in time to see his daughter regain consciousness and praised God that she was safe and sound. Master Adam wrapped a piece of cloth around my chest to contain the flow of blood. Sir Dominic's young squire Peter, asked his master whether they should pursue Cassandra and slay her.

"No, let her be for now, for she is beaten.

She is a mouse which scurries to its hole,

Humiliated, weak and having failed.

To kill her would be murder, and revenge

Belongs to God alone and not to us."

Sir Dominic embraced Rose tightly, and spoke to her with these soothing words:

"Beloved, thank the Lord that thou art safe."

He then turned to me and said,

"Dear Tristan, you are worthy of reward,

Your valour has preserved my darling's life."

"No sir," I said, bowing my head in shame. "I deserve to die, for I have betrayed you. Let me ask for forgiveness, receive the last rites and die."

"No, no, you shall not die, for you have shown

Great valour in the end, in saving Rose."

He paused and turned to his beloved Rose.

"How grieved thou must have been by me, my Rose,

Although it was not I who did all this,

But 'twas my foe, who somehow found a way

To fool thee into thinking she was I.

I came back to thy house to call for thee

Thy mother did inform me thou wast gone.

I asked her where, but she had no idea.

And what was strange was that Rose went with me.

I could not comprehend how this could be,

But sensed that something ill had come to pass.

I saw my servant's horse tied at a post

And noticed after that the footprints made

By that foul-smelling dung which stained his shoes!"

Sir Dominic could barely suppress his laugh as he pointed to my filthy shoes.

"Did you suspect that I betrayed you, sir?" I asked fearfully.

"In truth your absence troubled me and yet

I never thought you able to betray

Your friend who always puts his trust in you.

Forsooth, I thought my enemy did catch

And hold you captive, till you fought against her."

"In a certain way, she did hold me captive, sir. But in the end, I perceived her wickedness, and fought to defend your Rose."

"For that I am eternally in debt

To you, good Tristan, for your show of valour.

You shall be lavishly rewarded soon."

"But sir, I deserve no reward, truly. For it was because of me that Cassandra knew so much of Rose. She seduced me and extracted everything from my own foolish lips."

"All that shall be forgiven, have no fear.

For him who loved so much, as you have done,

So much shall be forgiven, faithful friend."

Rose was still crying with relief after the distressing incident that had just come to pass.

"My dearest knight, how sorely grieved I was

To see that cold impostor in thy form

How cruelly did he behave with me!

It must have been some demon out of hell!"

"Do dry thy tears, my dearest, all is well," said Sir Dominic, comforting her with tender kisses.

"For I, thy very Dominic, am here.
And never shall I let thee suffer aught
In future at the hands of my sworn foe.
Cassandra is intent to cause me harm
By causing harm to thee, my precious heart.
We must be vigilant, for she does prowl
A lioness enraged in search of prey.
Fear not, my precious flower, for I swear
I shall protect thee always, as I can.
And I should die before I let thee fall.
Let history record it in her pages,
I love thee with a love that spans the ages."

RESEARCHER'S NOTES

Cassandra went into hiding after that incident, and so did Tristan. Fearing for his life, he sought sanctuary in a monastery (probably following his friend Ludovic's advice), and used his master's reward to fund his travel to an abbey as far from Cambridge as possible. He journeyed to a monastery in Dublin, and was welcomed by Father Anthony, the abbot, and stayed until he took his holy orders and became a monk one year later. Once he became a monk, he wrote these confessions, as he explains in his first chapter. He explains in a later part of the text that his reason for writing these confessions was not only as an act of penance, but also in order to warn his young Christian brethren about the dangers of lust and seduction and of the dark, magical arts.

The rest of his text is mainly about procedures and protocols of the monastic order, which are not of much interest to the lay reader. But he does record that Cassandra made one more attempt to abduct Rose, and that Sir Dominic went in search of her, but he confesses that he knows little about this incident, because Sir Dominic did not divulge much about it.

Brother Benedict also reports that Cassandra must have left Cambridge and gone to live elsewhere, since no one knew where she was hiding, or whether she was still in England. Eventually, someone discovered where her house was, but it was vacant. The constable was notified, and he sent men to search the house from top to bottom. It took a while, but they eventually found the square that led to the basement. Once they were in the basement, they saw Cassandra's large mirror, by which she did all her magic, but it was cracked and inanimate. They collected many of her books, which they took back to the constable. He in turn took them to an exorcist, who examined them in detail and wrote a report on them before burning them. There were spells which dealt with shape changing, others which dealt with moving objects without touching them, others which provided recipes for mind altering drugs and potions, and others still which dealt with the mysteries of temporal displacement, or sending human beings to another time period.

There is a conclusion to the text, which supposedly includes another document, written in another person's handwriting, but I have not been able to find it. I have also been unable to find any mention of Sir Dominic's wedding to Rose. Further research needs to be done on this, and that will be the subject of another paper, at another conference in the near future.

END OF PART 1

~Part 2~

The Quest

(From the diary of Dr G. Arden, Ph.D. Cantab.)

SUNDAY 13 APRIL 2014 (DAY 1)

This is the day that has changed my life forever.

It was about 12:30 pm when I saw him. I was riding my bicycle in Rose Crescent, near St Michael's Court, when I noticed a peculiar sight: there was a man dressed in a mediaeval doublet and woollen hose and singing on the street. I naturally took him for an eccentric busker and went on my way, but when I heard what he was singing, I fell off my bicycle in surprise. He was actually singing in impeccable Middle English, and his text was from Chaucer's *Canterbury Tales*. When I fell, he stopped his singing and came to help me up.

"Sir, have you suffered any injury?"

I looked up and saw a young man in his early twenties, about six foot, well-built, with blue eyes, an aquiline nose, long dark brown hair and a beard. He reminded me of someone, but at the time, dazed and confused as I was by my fall, I could not recall who. At first I thought that he was just an eccentric busker with enormous talent, who must have studied Middle English at university and was capitalising on his talent. I looked in his hat, and the number of coins in there testified to the admiration of those passing by.

When he helped me up, I said to him, "I'm fine, thank you", but he looked at me with a quizzical expression on his face.

"Thank you, sir," I repeated as I stood on my feet again, "you are most kind. Allow me to introduce myself. My name is Dr Gabriel Arden, I am a professor of Mediaeval English literature at the University of Cambridge. And you are … ?"

As I spoke, the kind young man dressed in mediaeval clothing showed a total lack of comprehension. Perhaps he was a foreign student, I thought. So I made it easy for him. I held out my hand and said slowly, "My name is Dr Gabriel Arden. And you?"

The young man seemed to understand me this time, either because of the slower speech or because of my hand extended in expectation of a handshake.

"I am Sir Dominic Wright, a knight of Cambridge.
I come in search of my beloved Rose."

No way! Sure, he reminded me of Sir Dominic, because he matched the description of him in *The Confessions of Brother Benedict*, but there was no way in the world that a fifteenth century knight could just appear in twenty-first-century England. It was impossible! Perhaps this was a former student of mine, or a colleague who knew about my research, playing a prank, or perhaps he was a psychopath. But how could a student, a colleague or a psychopath speak perfect Middle English so poetically? Well, I knew that I had to be dealing with an expert mediaevalist who had done his homework. But why did he claim to be Sir Dominic of all people? Did he know that I was going to come by? I had a thousand questions swirling around in my brain, and I had to find answers.

Although I can comprehend fifteenth-century English quite well, being a professor of mediaeval English literature at the University of Cambridge, and having read and translated many manuscripts of the period, I have never been confident in speaking it. I have won many recital competitions in various earlier English pronunciations, but that is not the same as actually speaking to a person, having a conversation. But now I had to use it, if I was to find out anything about this eccentric young man who claimed to be Sir Dominic. I had to keep my wits about me and test him thoroughly.

"Sir", I started hesitantly, in the best Middle English accent I could muster, *"What brings you here?"*

I thought I would start with a general question first, to break the ice.

The young man looked at me with a more surprised look than I had when I fell off my bicycle. His eyes were wide open and his jaw dropped.

"Good sir, how is it that you speak like me?

All others speak a tongue quite strange to me.

What language do they speak in England now?"

"It is still English," I replied, *"but not as you know it. It has changed a lot."*

I paused, noticing the surprise still visible on his face.

Now for my next question: *"When were you born, sir?"*

"In AD thirteen hundred ninety-three
My mother brought me into life, then died.
My father raised me, with a nurse's aid
As well as my three sisters, as we grew,
Till I became a squire, then a knight."

Wow! He was good! How did he do his arithmetic so fast and work out Sir Dominic's correct year of birth? How did he present his answer so eloquently, so poetically, so spontaneously? Any student or teacher of Middle English who could do that would have to be a genius!

Still, I was not a hundred percent convinced. Call me a sceptic, but I still could not believe that it was Sir Dominic, although all the evidence was pointing in that direction. I needed more evidence.

Suddenly, I had an idea. I needed to record all this for historical purposes. It is not every day that one meets a mediaeval knight speaking poetically, or a consummate actor playing the part so well. This was a gem too precious to lose. I asked him to excuse me while I fumbled in my backpack and took out a small hand-held tape recorder. I already had a tape there from a previous interview with a university scholar. I pressed the record button and tied the device to my belt, as mediaeval people used to tie purses and weapons to theirs.

The young man was baffled by all of this, but I told him not to worry about it. And as for ethical concerns and privacy laws, if he really were Sir Dominic from the fifteenth century, what would he know about all of that?

"Do not worry," I assured him. *"This is a device from our era, that we use to record what people say, for posterity. I need to record your speech, because this is all too incredible for words."*

The young man nodded and said,

"Then let your scribe inside the box record
My words, if this will help you to believe.
I understand full well your doubts, good sir.
These circumstances are quite strange indeed.
Be patient, and with time you shall believe
That I am who I say I am, a knight
In search of his affianced damsel, Rose.
Believe me for my words, or else believe
Because of actions that you see me do.
Pray ask me anything, and by my troth
You shall receive the answers that you seek."

Now I was really stunned. This man must be Sir Dominic, incredible as it was. He looked like Sir Dominic, spoke like Sir Dominic, and claimed to be Sir Dominic. Although I still had some burning questions, I had to give him the benefit of the doubt.

Now it was his turn to ask a question.

"Sir, could you tell me in what year we are?"

"Yes", I replied, *"this is 2014 (two thousand and fourteen). It is the 13 April, to be exact."*

"So then I have but six mere days to find her."

He looked pensive and remained silent. I was not sure whether he was thinking or praying.

I was aware that some people were staring at us, but no one disturbed us. That is typical of the twenty-first century: no one wants to get involved in anyone's business; it's not safe. But that suited us fine. Anyway, what was so odd about a university professor of English literature interviewing what appeared to be an actor for a stage or film production of one of the great literary works?

In any case, just to avoid unnecessary attention, I encouraged Sir Dominic to come with me to a quieter place, where we could talk in peace. He agreed, gathered the earnings that he made from singing (a total of one shilling, six pence—a considerable amount in his day), and came with me.

As we made our way to my flat near the university (slowly, because I was walking my bicycle beside me), Sir Dominic looked around in wonder at his surroundings and at the people that he saw in the streets. He made comments to me about many things, and I nodded, knowing how strange it must all appear to him. He marvelled that no one carried a weapon as he did, that a few closed carriages moved without horses, that many people rode on strange machines with two wheels (like my bicycle), and that people appeared to be talking to themselves while holding their ears (actually they were talking on small mobiles). He also noticed that most of the buildings that he knew in his own time were still standing, including the university of course, and many, but not all, of the churches. Then he said, with a hint of despair,

"How shall I ever find my Rose in time?
I only have six days in this large town."

There! He said it again: six days. What did he mean? I was dying to find out.

When we entered my flat, I told Sir Dominic to be comfortable and I served him a cup of tea. I was not sure whether he would like it, because he certainly did not have any in 1414, but it was always good to try new things. I then went to my study and searched for the original manuscript of *The Confessions of Brother Benedict* and brought it into the living room.

"Sir Dominic, you may be surprised, but I actually know you, in a way. To know why, I think you ought to read this. I'm sure that you are familiar with this story. After all, it's all about you and Rose Thorne."

"You mean to say that you do know my Rose?

Pray tell me where she is, I need to know."

"I know not where she is any more than you, but I know your story."

I pushed the manuscript closer to him and urged him to read it.

"And I really want to help you, as much as I can," I said sincerely.

"Thank God for you, kind sir, I say in truth.

The Lord in bounteous grace brought you to me."

"I wouldn't go that far!" I replied modestly.

Sir Dominic delayed no further and started to read the document. It surprised me that he read aloud, but I remembered that reading silently to oneself was not common in the Middle Ages. I sat opposite him, drinking my tea and watching his reactions as he read. I was mesmerised as I sat listening to him speaking the words of the original so mellifluously. He was so engrossed in his reading that he forgot all about his tea, which became cold and had to be thrown out. Anyway, anyone can imagine Sir Dominic's reactions to the story by reading the Confessions from his point of view.

After he read the document, he sat quietly for a moment, and then spoke,

*"My good friend Tristan tells a moving tale
He makes it fresh and lively, so much so
It feels like only yesterday although
It came to pass now nigh on two good months."*

I suppressed a laugh at his perception of time. "Two good months" for him, about six hundred more years for me!

"Sir Dominic, you know now how I learned about you and your story, as far as your friend tells it, but there is no mention of how you came here, although Brother Benedict mentions that Cassandra tried to abduct Rose once more, and that you went in search of her."

*"Yea, this is what has now occurred and why
I came to find my Rose in the age to come."*

Aha! Now things are falling into place!

I asked Sir Dominic to tell the story, so he proceeded to narrate how he, his squire Peter and Master Adam escorted Rose and Madam Eveline her mother to the markets in town on Friday 13 April 1414.

Friday 13 April! How did he know that 13 April in 1414 was a Friday? I excused myself for a second, saying that I had to go to the "privy" (the toilet), but there, in privacy, I checked with Google on my mobile, and the day of 13 April 1414 was indeed a Friday! I gasped, but suppressed the sound, for fear that Sir Dominic might hear me. If I needed any more evidence that this man was Sir Dominic from the fifteenth century, this was it! I came out of the toilet and asked Sir Dominic to resume his narration.

He told me that they passed a dress shop on Rose Crescent (strange coincidence with the name!), and Rose wished to enter to look at wedding gowns for her impending nuptials. The seamstress standing at the door of the shop seemed a kind and welcoming woman, who knew by uncanny instinct that Rose needed a wedding gown and encouraged her to enter and sample her wares. Madam Eveline, wary of leaving her daughter alone after what had happened previously, went in with Rose.

Sir Dominic, Peter and Master Adam walked on ahead, looking at other shops and discussing court affairs and politics. After a short time (something like half an hour), Madam Eveline came running out of the shop, all bleeding, with scratches and bruises to the head. Master Adam promptly attended to her wounds as she told them how she had entered the shop with Rose, who started to try on every gown that she saw. Eventually, Rose found one that she really liked. The seamstress gently guided her to the mirror, to let her see what she looked like with the gown on. Then the seamstress said something in Latin, which neither Madam Eveline nor Rose understood fully, but the phrase "sex saecula" stuck in the mother's mind. Then an extraordinary thing happened: the mirror's glass seemed to turn into water and the seamstress pushed Rose in! Rose was there one second, and then she was not! Madam Eveline screamed but the seamstress quickly put a hand over her mouth. Madam Eveline bit the seamstress' hand, but the latter struck her on the cheek with one hand and scratched her other cheek with the other hand. Madam Eveline screamed at the seamstress, demanding to know where Rose was. The seamstress laughed and said that Rose was far away and would never come back.

Madam Eveline, in desperation, fought and struggled with the seamstress, demanding that she bring Rose back or else be burnt at the stake as a witch. The seamstress, who obviously was Cassandra, positively cackled, then said the same words about "sex saecula" and disappeared into the mirror herself. Madam Eveline, once she recovered, told the men what had happened, so Sir Dominic, his squire and Master Adam rushed to the dress shop to see all this for themselves.

They saw the mirror, which was as tall as a person, standing against the wall at the back of the shop. Sir Dominic stepped forward to face the mirror and addressed it in Latin, commanding it to take him to Rose. Nothing happened. Then Sir Dominic started to pray in Latin, and the mirror started to hiss and emit smoke (It's all smoke and mirrors with Cassandra!). Sir Dominic continued his prayer, and the mirror screamed *"SATIS!"* ("Enough!"). The mirror then said that Sir Dominic could go after Rose but under one condition, which it gave in Latin. The English translation would render it thus:

"One day for every hundred years
For every hundred years one day.
Will your quest end in joy or tears?
True love alone will find the way."

Sir Dominic, addressing the mirror, spoke these words solemnly:

"Then so be it! I shall go after Rose
And rescue her wherever she may be.
O mirror, take me where my Rose is gone
For I shall bring her back if God so wills."

Rose's parents had tears in their eyes and urged him to bring their daughter back safe and sound. Peter begged Sir Dominic to let him come too, but the reply was negative.

"I thank you for your loyalty and courage
But sadly, I must tread this path alone."

Sir Dominic waved to them, made the sign of the cross, stepped into the liquefied glass and disappeared from their sight.

So here was Sir Dominic Wright of Cambridge, on a quest to find and rescue his beloved bride-to-be, Rose Thorne, and he came all the way into the year 2014 to do it.

We had to think of a strategy. We had no picture of Rose to post on telegraph poles with the words 'Have you seen this woman?'. Sir Dominic suggested that we search around Rose Crescent for anyone who had seen anything suspicious earlier today. One could not have missed a young blonde woman with long hair down to the small of her back, appearing out of nowhere in a wedding gown and looking all confused. So we decided that that was the best course of action to take—and hoped that Cassandra had not already found her first.

In order not to be too conspicuous this time, I offered Sir Dominic one of my jackets, and he left his sword in my flat. I assured him that no one would challenge him to a duel in this day and age, and that we had police, a sort of team of law enforcing knights or soldiers, to administer justice.

We then went around the area, but no one seemed to know anything about Rose. Some people remembered a young, blonde woman in a white formal gown, but to them, she was just another young woman going to church or coming out of one. After all, it was Palm Sunday today, an important date in the Christian calendar, apparently. We kept asking, and we spent nearly an hour and a half doing so, until one lady told us that she saw someone matching our description.

"Where did she go?" I asked, excitedly. "Did you see where she went, Madam?"

"Well, up to a point, yes," she replied. "She wandered around this street, looking around her, and she seemed quite distressed. She wandered around looking for something, and saw Great St Mary's Church over there and started making her way towards it in a hurry. That's all I know, sorry."

"Thank you, Madam. You've been a great help."

I translated for Sir Dominic, but he seemed to have got the gist of the conversation by himself.

We approached Great St Mary's Church, or The Church of St Mary the Great, as it is otherwise known. Sir Dominic recognised it, since it already existed in his day. We asked some more passers-by whether they had seen Rose.

One elderly gentleman, who was sitting on a bench told us that he saw a young, blonde woman in distress approach Great St Mary's, but that a young lady coming out of the same church saw her and went to her aid. Sir

Dominic, who seemed to understand more than I thought he would, breathed a sigh of relief. The elderly gentleman said that the kind young lady helped the distressed one, tried to communicate with her but could not, and then gently escorted her somewhere else. Unfortunately, all that he could say about the helpful young lady was that she was about 30 years old, short with brown hair. We thanked him and continued on our way, and then Sir Dominic said,

"The maiden who escorted Rose away
Came out from this great church; so Rose is safe.
Cassandra, as you know, would never enter
A house of worship, for she is a witch.
I now have faith that we shall surely find
My precious Rose, who now is in safe hands."

Sir Dominic was right. Now we had to find the young lady who found Rose and took her home.

We tried the church itself as a last resort. There was no one there at the time, since it was mid-afternoon, so we went to the rectory. The minister, Reverend Christopher, was a young man who was slightly balding, and after staring at Sir Dominic, asked us how he could help. I introduced Sir Dominic Wright to him as a friend, without the title, and told him that we were looking for a short young lady with brown hair who helped a young blonde lady outside his church. He laughed good-naturedly, saying that many young women matched that description, but that he could not remember seeing or hearing anything strange.

"I'll keep a look out for you," he promised, as we thanked him and took our leave.

We were heading back to my flat when we heard someone call out my name. It was Oscar Giles, one of my friends from our undergraduate days, who is now running his own online business. I greeted him politely, and introduced him to Sir Dominic, but as a friend from abroad.

"Hey, that's cool!" said Oscar, shaking his hand. "Nice to meet you, mate!"

Sir Dominic smiled and nodded, but said nothing.

"Hey, Gabe, mate," he said, turning to me, "I'm going down to the Fountain tonight. Do you wanna come? There's this cool new band playing, you've got to see them!"

"No thanks, Oscar, I have a busy day tomorrow, so I need to retire to bed early tonight. Perhaps another time?"

"Sure, mate, no problem. It's all good. Say, where did you meet this new mate of yours? Dom, is it?"

"Ah … Dominic is … a … student who … is doing some research on … the *Romance of the Rose*", I lied, improvising as I went along.

"Oh, one of your fancy-pants uni research projects again? That's cool. It's all good, mate. I'll leave you to it. Cheers!"

He shook hands with both of us before running off to a nearby café.

Sir Dominic and I went home and rested, preparing ourselves for the day ahead. I noticed that he stood beside my bed (I opted for the couch) and said his prayers in Latin and English before sleeping. I went to the study and used the recordings which I made to write the recount of the day. I want to record as much of this as possible, because it is not every day that a mediaeval knight visits you to ask for your help on a quest.

MONDAY 14 APRIL 2014 (DAY 2)

I had no idea until yesterday and this morning how many daily activities and procedures I have been taking for granted. I had to show Sir Dominic how we take baths and showers, how we brush our teeth, how we use the toilet, how we shave, how we prepare breakfast, how we use kitchen appliances, how we entertain ourselves with television and the Internet, and many, many more things. Sir Dominic did expect things to be different but he marvelled at all the technological changes that have taken place since his time.

"You have this wonderful device which lets
One reach a friend by voice from far away.
And this great mirror hanging on your wall
Allows you to behold worldwide events.
Pray tell me, is this all by sorcery?
Or has the Lord bestowed upon mankind
The power to perform these wondrous works?"

I explained to him that the latter was probably true, although my faith in God is not as strong as his. Frankly, I have never before contemplated how marvellous our everyday appliances and technology are; I just took them for granted like everyone else. But when you come from a world where the most advanced technology consists of gunpowder and spectacles, and the rest is witchcraft in their eyes, you see everything from a different perspective—almost like a child.

Now Sir Dominic was not the only person surprised by our six hundred year difference in culture: I also, despite my extensive study into the literature of the period, am surprised by Sir Dominic's piety. Yes, I have always known that the church played a greater role in people's daily lives in the Middle Ages, but I always thought that people just paid lip-service to it; I did not expect that people actually took it seriously. And I knew that Sir Dominic prayed occasionally, because it was recorded in the *Confessions of Brother Benedict*, but again, I thought that he prayed for God to help him in a crisis. But from what I have seen, Sir Dominic prays a lot, and in Latin! He prays before sleeping at night, he prays in the morning, he prays before eating, he prays after eating. I am not very comfortable with it, but I respect his devotion.

Sir Dominic and I talked a lot this morning, and I told him how much I admire him, and how much I love his era. In fact, I opened up to him and told him how I would have loved to live in the Middle Ages rather than now. In the Middle Ages, there was chivalry, respect, excitement, nobility, heroism and valour. People spoke a purer, richer and more poetic form of English, as Sir Dominic does.

There were fewer people around, so everyone was important and significant. In my time, there are so many people around that no one cares about my achievements, no one knows about my scholarship. I am a professor at a prestigious English university, but no one seems to care or know that I exist, apart from my family. I live alone, and I have friends that I can count on my fingers; I do the same thing day in and day out; I have no quest or purpose in life; I do not really follow any religion, although I was born Christian. So what is the meaning of my life? Why am I here? Why was I not born in the Middle Ages or the Renaissance, when literature, academic learning and culture flourished? What culture is there now, outside of my ivory tower of Cambridge University? Who has read my doctoral thesis or papers, apart from the academic staff?

Sir Dominic listened patiently as I poured my feelings out, fully aware that I needed a friend who would listen to me. After I finished, he put his hand on my shoulder and said,

'My friend, be not upset about your fate.
The Lord above does not do any wrong.
He planted you in this age for a reason.
His plan for you is purposeful and right.
Why do you look regretfully behind
And wish that you had grown up in my time?
My era had so many awful times
Of war, of danger, pestilence and death,
Which far outnumber times of peace and joy.
Behold your time: the many wonders here
That people in my time could not conceive!
You live in peace and comfort every day

You have good food and health and live so long.
So be content that God has put you here.
You shall discover soon why this is so.
Now be content to bloom where you are planted
And thank God for the blessings you are granted."

I thanked him for his good advice and suggested that we devise a strategy for finding the young lady who found Rose and took her home, but we were interrupted by a telephone call on my mobile. I smiled as I saw the incredulity in Sir Dominic's eyes.

"Hello? Dr Gabriel Arden speaking."

"Hi, Gabe mate!" said the familiar voice of my friend Oscar. "How's it hanging?"

I listened patiently as Oscar talked about everything and nothing, his speech peppered with slang. He mainly talked about his night out yesterday at the restaurant and night club known as The Fountain.

"Hey mate, I met this really hot bird last night at the club. We hit it off from the get go. We danced like crazy, then I took her to my place and we—"

"Thank you, Oscar, I don't need to hear the details. I get the picture. So tell me, what's her name?"

"Well, I didn't quite catch it: Sam or Sally—no! Sandy! Yes, that's it! Sandy. I'll ask her next time I see her and I'll tell you on Facebook, ok?"

"Sure," I said, weary of hearing about another of Oscar's sexual conquests.

"She's hot, mate! You've got to meet her! She doesn't speak English well, though. I think she's Dutch or something. But that's cool, because she knows how to—"

"Oscar, do you always think with your—" I paused, aware that Sir Dominic was listening, and subconsciously felt the need to change my choice of words, like someone who feels naked in front of a baby. "Are you always so carnally minded? You can enjoy those private details by yourself. I'm sorry, but I have to go now."

"Gabe mate, when are you going to get a girl? Come on, you've got to leave those books and come out with me more often! I'll find you a bird—unless …"

I was becoming irritated now. I knew where this was going. Oscar has always doubted my heterosexual preference.

"Unless you prefer the blokes. I saw you with a tall bloke yesterday, and I was wondering …"

"Oscar, for the last time, I AM NOT GAY!" I shouted in exasperation. "That 'bloke' is a good friend of mine, who is looking for his sweetheart, a young woman, I'll have you know. I will not have you—"

"All right, all right, calm down, old chap! I was just worried about you, mate."

"For your information, just because a man is not sexually involved with a woman doesn't make him gay."

"That's not an 'Arden fast rule'!" he said, chuckling with self-satisfaction at his witless sense of humour. He meant "hard and fast rule", of course, but he likes to pun on my name.

"Look, Oscar, thank you, but don't worry about me, all right? I'm fine."

"Ok, I'll talk to you later, mate. Sandy's coming over soon."

After I hung up, Sir Dominic asked me with a tone of concern,

"I heard that you are not a cheerful man.
Your friend appears to vex you with his talk."

"Not cheerful? No, he just annoyed me, that's all. He just thinks that when he finds a new girl, and that's like once a week, he has to tell everyone about it. I am used to it now. But I can be cheerful. I am happy now when I am talking to you."

After hearing myself say those words aloud, I understood what Sir Dominic meant. He must have heard me shout "I am not gay" and concluded that I was an unhappy person. I explained to him that some words have changed their meaning and that the beautiful, poetic, melodious language of the fifteenth century was no more. Sir Dominic nodded sadly, and said,

"It is indeed a pity when we hear
Some people speak with coarse or vulgar words.
It hurts our ears and brings our spirits down.
But verily, vulgarity is old
And in my time it was around as well.
Man can employ his gift of speech for good
Or evil, if his heart is full thereof.
And this is true for your time and for mine."

While we were walking back towards Rose Crescent, Sir Dominic thought that he saw Rose from behind. The blonde girl of about eighteen years of age was accompanied by another young lady who was short with brown hair. They matched our description. I approached them and said,

"Excuse me, young ladies," I said to both and then turned my gaze to the blonde girl, "My friend and I are looking for a beautiful girl called Rose Thorne. We were wondering if that's you". The blonde girl looked at us, eyed Sir Dominic up and down, turned to her friend and burst out laughing. Then her friend laughed too. Then they walked off, still laughing, without even saying goodbye or excusing themselves.

Sir Dominic turned to me and said,

"I know not why those maidens were uncivil.
For rarely have I seen such disrespect
From anyone, be he a friend or foe.
Although we seemed unusual to them,
They could at least have answered yes or no
And we should have continued on our way.
Pray tell, are all the people of today
As cold and disrespectful as those two?"

"It is a long story, Sir Dominic, and far too difficult to explain. You are probably better off not knowing about it."

How could I explain to Sir Dominic that young people did not respect their elders as they used to, or that young women did not hold the same respect towards young men?

I took Sir Dominic to some clothes shops, in order to buy him some contemporary clothes, because I feared that he appeared too conspicuous, or dare I say ridiculous, in mediaeval clothes, even with the jacket over them. He settled on a shirt and black trousers. After we left that shop, people stopped staring at us, and no one laughed at us anymore.

As the day wore on, Sir Dominic appeared more and more downcast. I turned to him and tried to be positive.

"Cheer up, Sir Dominic. I know that you will find Rose before your time is up. We just have to keep trying. According to what people have been saying, the young lady took Rose to these parts, near Trinity Lane. We shall probably find her around here."

"Not probably, dear sir, we have to find her!" said Sir Dominic with fierce determination.

"And find her we shall!" I replied, as positively as I could.

As we went to lunch at a nearby café, and after I showed him how to use a fork and introduced him to our strange cuisine, (compared to mediaeval food and drink , that is), we talked about our lives. I was so impressed with his faith in God in every matter and circumstance. My faith is not as strong as his, as I have said earlier, even though I have always been influenced by the great Christian writers of English literature. I confessed to Sir Dominic that I do not believe God to be working in this age or showing any signs or miracles as he used to. I am not an atheist, but I feel that God has forsaken this generation. Life seems so dull and mundane, and everyone seems so distant. Sir Dominic tried to explain how great God is, allowing him, a mortal, to thwart Cassandra's witchcraft and cross several centuries to search for his beloved. He also praises God for allowing him to meet Rose in the first place and win her love. I nodded politely and said, "I suppose so", but I am still not convinced.

"Then wait and see the wonders still to come!" said Sir Dominic confidently.

"The Lord does work in great, mysterious ways
His wonders to perform in His good time."

As we walked through the streets of Cambridge, Sir Dominic asked me about my life, whether there was any "maiden" that I loved. I said that there was not, unfortunately, but that I once knew a girl, a "maiden", at university, not long ago. She used to be a student who attended my lectures, before I obtained my doctorate. She had the most profound respect for me and my scholarship, and listened to me avidly. After she graduated (with first class honours), she still attended all my conferences and read all my papers, even those about the *Confessions of Brother Benedict*. After one of those conferences, I gave her my number for her to contact me by telephone (I reminded Sir Dominic what that was) and have some more discussions over a drink and something to eat ("coffee" was too hard to explain). I explained that she also gave me her telephone number, and asked me to do the same. But I have not seen or heard from her since Christmas last year, when she told me that she was going on holidays abroad to see her relatives.

As we entered my flat again, and sat down, Sir Dominic asked me,

"But why did you not call her as she asked?"

"I was waiting for her to call me first," I replied, as if it were the most natural reason in the world.

"I may not be familiar with your customs,
In this late age, so different from my own,
But in my day, it was up to the man
To take the lead and call upon the maid (girl)."

"You are right, Sir Dominic, I know. But I guess I have just been too shy to call."

Sir Dominic was silent for awhile, and so was I, until we were interrupted in our thoughts by a beeping sound. It was a text message on my mobile. Sir Dominic was naturally surprised by the "internal bell heralding new tidings in my minute engine (device)." But it was my turn to be surprised when I read the text:

"DR. ARDEN, HAVE YOU CHECKED YOUR E-MAIL LATELY?"

It was from a number that I did not recognise. I took my tablet computer and checked my e-mail, and saw Sir Dominic's look of surprise (he must have thought that it was a magic mirror!), but it was not as great as mine! The e-mail was from Georgina Olivet, the very girl about whom we had just been talking! It was dated 13 April, and the time it was sent was 9 pm. Here is what it said:

"Dear Dr Arden,

Please call me on the number below. I have something very important to tell you. Frankly it is unbelievable!

Yours faithfully,

Georgina Olivet

(Your former student)"

I have to admit, I was now starting to doubt my sanity. The coincidence, nay the whole situation, was too incredible for words. Here was Sir Dominic, a fifteenth-century knight, telling me to contact a "maiden" with whom I had been infatuated, but whom I lacked the courage to call. And then the same "maiden" herself asks me to call her! Maybe miracles do happen after all.

Nervously, I dialled the number on my home telephone, my hand shaking. The dial tone signalled that she was available. Then "click"! She answered!

"Hello? Georgina Olivet speaking."

"Uh … uh … Good evening, Miss Olivet, this is Dr Gabriel Arden."

"Oh hello, Dr Arden".

I liked how she pronounced my surname: she rolled the R ("Arrrden"), which is something my other friends, colleagues or family members do not do. It kind of kills my name when it is pronounced "Ahden" all the time.

"I need to tell you something, Dr Arden. You have read my e-mail, haven't you?"

"Yes, that's why I'm calling you …"

"Before we begin, professor, why have you waited until now to call me?"

"I'm so sorry, I was busy yesterday when you sent it. I only saw it today, a few minutes ago actually, after you sent the text …"

"No, professor, I mean why have you waited until now, and didn't call me for four months?"

I was tongue-tied. How do I answer that? I was so embarrassed.

"Anyway, professor, enough of that now. Are you sitting down?"

I sat down.

"Yes, but you don't need to call me 'professor' or 'Dr Arden' anymore," I said. "You are no longer my student. Just call me Gabriel."

"Gabriel," she started hesitatingly, uncomfortable with the new level of familiarity, "I have found a young lady who seems to have come out of one of your mediaeval manuscripts …"

I fell off my chair.

"Are you all right, professor? Professor? Gabriel? Have you fallen down? Are you ill?"

"Rose Thorne? Have you found Rose Thorne?"

"How did you … ? Yes, I found a young lady of about seventeen or eighteen who answers to the name of Rose Thorne. She is tall, with long, blond hair down to the middle of her back, blue eyes, she speaks an older form of English …"

"Yes, that is she! You have found Rose Thorne!"

"Thanks be to God in heaven! Rose is safe!" exclaimed Sir Dominic, drawing closer and listening attentively. It is safe to say that he understood the gist of what I was saying!

"How did you find her?" I asked.

"I can tell you that when we meet. Relax, she is in good hands. I have been taking care of her since about eleven o'clock yesterday morning."

So Georgina was the young lady who escorted Rose to her home yesterday! Talk about being in the right place at the right time! I call it an amazing coincidence, but I suppose that Sir Dominic would call it a miracle.

"This is incredible, Georgina! We have no time to waste! We have to bring this couple back together as soon as possible. When and where can we meet?"

"How about nine tomorrow morning, outside Great St Mary's Church? Is that all right with you?"

"Certainly! They can reunite and break the spell and return to their own time!"

"Sorry, I don't quite understand."

"I'll explain tomorrow. See you at nine outside Great St Mary's Church."

After that telephone call, I was so excited about the prospect of helping Sir Dominic and Rose to reunite that I did not at first realise how attracted I am becoming to Georgina. What a sweet, delicious voice she has!

TUESDAY 15 APRIL 2014 (DAY 3)

At nine on the dot, Sir Dominic and I met Georgina outside Great St Mary's Church. Georgina and I shook hands, and I introduced her to Sir Dominic.

"So you are Sir Dominic! I have read so much about you!"

"I am so pleased to meet you too, dear Madam."

"What a gentleman you are!" said Georgina smiling, impressed with his bow and graceful salutation.

"Did you understand him?" I asked, quite impressed.

"Yes, I got the gist!" laughed Georgina. "Have you forgotten that I studied English literature with you as my lecturer?"

"Yes, how silly of me!"

"Don't say that! You are not silly. Now Professor—I mean Gabriel—please translate for Sir Dominic that I found Rose two days ago, wandering around aimlessly near here, dressed in a simple white wedding gown and sobbing. I was coming out of church that morning. When I saw her and went up to her, I asked her what was wrong, but she did not understand me. I thought that she was a foreign student, obviously running away from someone, maybe from her groom! I had no idea who she was, really."

"I don't blame you! All of this seems too incredible for words!"

"Exactly! Who would believe all this?"

Then she paused until I translated the gist to Sir Dominic, but he seemed to have already understood more of the conversation than we expected. After all, Georgina, whose first language is not English, speaks with a clear accent, pronouncing almost every vowel and consonant with the utmost purity. If accents were flavours of dessert, hers would be crunchy honeycomb.

Georgina continued, oblivious to my growing admiration for her.

"I tried to talk to her as I would talk to lost children, and she understood when I introduced myself and asked for her name. Even when she said "Rose", I did not realise that she was Sir Dominic's Rose, how could I? Besides, Rose is a common name these days. I noticed that she had an accent that sounded a bit French, so I thought that she was originally French. My flatmate Veronica speaks fluent French, so I thought she might help. But as we walked along towards my flat, Rose started to cry, telling me over and over again that she was lost, and asking where her mother was. I realised then that she knew English, but I thought that she was a foreigner with an unusual accent. I put my arm around her shoulder to comfort her until we reached my flat.

I introduced her to Veronica and she tried to speak French with Rose, but turned to me and said, 'I have never heard this dialect of French before: it sounds like a Canadian or New Orleans creole.' I said that I found her English a bit unusual too."

As Georgina was speaking, I watched Sir Dominic nod and show avid interest in what she was saying.

"It did not hit me straight away," continued Georgina, "but by the evening, I realised that she was Rose Thorne. What eventually gave it away was when I realised that her pronunciation of English was like the Middle English that I learned in your course, professor, and the fact that she kept asking herself where Sir Dominic Wright was, praying and sobbing continuously."

"Yes, that last clue would give it away!" I said laughing.

"All the evidence pointed in that direction, but I refused to believe it at first. It seemed impossible! I had to test my hypothesis. I asked her what the names of her father and mother were. She hesitated, and I hoped that she understood. She answered, "Master Adam and Madam Eveline Thorne". That's when I wrote you an e-mail, profess ... Gabriel. Rose then went to have a rest, Veronica went out to do something or other ..."

"Did Rose tell you how she came here?" I asked.

"Yes. She said that she went to a dress shop with her mother, and the last thing she remembers was looking into the mirror in the wedding gown that she was trying on. Then she found herself here, where no one understood her, before she met me."

77

"Yes, and she headed for the nearest church for sanctuary. She saw this church from where she was and ran here, right?"

"Yes, Gabriel. That is correct."

"And you were coming out of the church and saw her and went to help her straight away?"

"Yes, poor soul! My heart ached for her."

Then Sir Dominic turned to Georgina and asked her a question that was troubling him over the last few minutes.

"Did anybody see you when you met my Rose?"

I was about to translate, but Georgina indicated to me by her facial expression that she understood.

"Sure", she replied, "many people. It was Sunday morning, Palm Sunday in fact. The place was crowded. Do you mean anyone in particular?"

I was amazed how quickly Sir Dominic had adjusted to our modern dialect, but that is probably thanks to Georgina's beautiful, clear and foreign-sounding pronunciation.

"I fear Cassandra might have seen you two."

"Yes," I said, *"That is possible. I did not think of that.* Georgina, remember, from the *Confessions of Brother Benedict*, that witch Cassandra, who tried to fool Rose and kill her, but was thwarted by Tristan? According to Sir Dominic, she followed Rose into our era, but not straight away; she was delayed. But she might have seen you and followed you."

Georgina now looked worried.

"I did not notice anyone following me on Sunday, but yesterday, I saw the caretaker of my building looking at me in a strange way. And this morning, as I was coming out of my flat, a middle-aged woman looked at me in a strange way before going into the toilets."

I looked at Sir Dominic and he looked at me, each of us as worried as the other. We understood with our eyes what the danger was.

"Georgina", I said urgently, "we don't have a moment to lose! We must hurry back to your flat immediately!"

We ran back to Georgina's flat as quickly as possible, but unfortunately, we were too late: Rose was not there!

"Veronica!" cried Georgina to her flatmate. "Where is Rose?"

"She went with her mother," answered Veronica, as if it were the most natural thing in the world.

"Her mother!" I exclaimed. "That's impossible."

Sir Dominic understood and buried his face in his hands.

"Why? What's the problem?" asked Veronica. "Her mother knocked on the door, about five minutes after you left, Georgina. When I opened the door, Rose saw her and ran to her, cried "Mama", and embraced her. They said some things to each other which I could not understand, but Rose turned around to me and explained, in her strange French creole, that her mother had finally come for her, promising to take her to her fiancé Sir Dominic. I said 'alright' and let them go."

"Don't blame yourself, Veronica, you were not to know," explained Georgina gently, "but that woman was not really Rose's mother."

"Because Rose's mother was left behind in 1414," I added. "Sir Dominic came alone."

"Can someone please tell me what's going on?" asked Veronica, with a look on her face that screamed that everyone was raving mad.

"I'll explain it to you later, if you will believe me," Georgina reassured her.

I looked at Sir Dominic, who had been silent all this time. He was praying, with his head bowed and his eyes closed. But it was too late. What could prayer do for him now, since Rose was lost again?

"So who was the woman that Rose thought was her mother?" asked Georgina. "Was it—"

"Cassandra the witch," I said, sure of myself. "Do you remember how she devised spells for disguising herself? Well, she is doing it again. I suspect that she has been following all our movements since—since Rose, and then Sir Dominic, appeared in our time."

"This is too much for me!" moaned Veronica. "I'm going to my room to study. See you all later."

We said 'See you later' too, and she retired to her room. Georgina went to the kitchen. Sir Dominic finished his prayer and made the sign of the cross.

"What use is your prayer now?" I asked him. *"We have to locate Cassandra now before she kills Rose."*

"My dear professor, may I say just this?
Our Lord did say that faith can move all mountains.
Cassandra shall not lay a hand on Rose
To harm or kill her, she must lack the courage
With all these people present. And she lacks
A secret lair to do her dirty deeds.
In truth I say, Cassandra has to find
A friend in Cambridge to assist her now

80

For she intends to keep dear Rose imprisoned
Until I come to seek her; she hates me
And wills that I should never marry Rose.
I know that one of these days, if need be
I shall confront Cassandra, if God wills."

"*If you say so,*" I replied. "*Your faith never ceases to amaze me, Sir Dominic. Well, I suppose you are right. Let me get this straight: Cassandra hates you more than she hates Rose. She wants to hurt you more than she wants to hurt her. I do not think that cold-blooded murder is part of her plan. Perhaps it is because she lacks the courage, perhaps because she takes a vain pleasure in using magic. In the past, she has always tried to use deception, with her mirrors and her attempts at abduction, including this forced exile in another time. Her main aim is to keep you and Rose apart, to prevent your marriage, not to kill.*"

"*Good doctor, you are wise beyond your years,*" replied Sir Dominic, smiling.

"*How well you understand this woman's mind!*
And you have never met her, as I have,
But gathered information from your text."

"*I am honoured by your praise, sir,*" I said, immensely flattered that this great and noble knight was saying such wonderful things about me. No one has ever sung my praises like that before. I am used to applause and "positive feedback" from my peers and students, but nothing this sincere from someone so worthy. A million insincere words of commendation are not worth one sincere word from someone of Sir Dominic's calibre.

Georgina let us stay for awhile in her flat, and she cooked for us all an excellent midday meal of chicken and rice, which even Sir Dominic enjoyed. We then talked a lot about university, English literature and the twenty-first century, and even explained to him how our dialect of English differs from his. He was already aware that many of the vowel sounds, especially the long ones, are pronounced differently, and that most people in South East England, except people like Georgina, for whom English is a second language, do not pronounce the R after vowels. He was also aware that we have not preserved the important distinction between *thou* and *you*, which not only distinguished singular from plural but also highlighted social relationships between speakers. I explained to him that the pronunciation, vocabulary and grammar started to change a lot later in his century, and that the printing press, invented a few decades after he left his time, would revolutionise mass communication and the dissemination of language.

"So man has made great strides in all the arts
In these six hundred years, thanks be to God."

"Yes," I replied, *"but not many people think that God has anything to do with it."*

This seemed to baffle Sir Dominic.

"I cannot comprehend, in this new age of science
Of "mass communication", as you say,
Why people have less faith in God in heaven
And seem so cold and distant to each other."

Sir Dominic and I turned in amazement towards Georgina. It was she who added this thought in verse, but in Modern English. I had my mouth open in wonder longer than Sir Dominic, who smiled. Georgina laughed and said,

"Pray close your mouth, professor, for the flies

May enter and remain to taste your words!"

After talking for another hour or so about mediaeval times and customs, Sir Dominic and I returned to my flat.

Not much else has happened today. Sir Dominic is sure that Rose is still alive, somewhere, and that he will soon find her. He is certain that Cassandra is using her to cause the maximum pain to him, and that Rose is more useful to her alive. Sir Dominic assured me on the way home that he is determined to rescue Rose, even if it costs him his life, but he says his time has not yet come. I'm glad that he has that faith, because frankly, I have my doubts.

After Sir Dominic retired to bed, and I finished recording the day's events, I turned on my computer to do some research. Before that, I played a game of chess to relax my nerves. I played black (which appears as red on the screen), and the computer played white. I lost in the end, but the way in which I lost was interesting. Early in the game, I captured the white queen and was in the lead, but White checkmated me by forking my queen and king with his knight; in other words, putting my king in check while attacking my queen simultaneously. Could this be a sign that Sir Dominic, the "White Knight", although his White Queen has been captured, will eventually defeat the Red(-haired) Queen? Look at me now! Sir Dominic's belief in miracles is having an effect on me! I am seeing a prophetic message in a game of chess!

On a different note, I am falling in love with Georgina. She is so intelligent, so good at understanding different dialects (even across the ages!) and so kind and respectful towards me. She has never once spoken impolitely or disrespectfully towards me or Sir Dominic, as Cassandra once did, six hundred years ago, to Sir Dominic and his household. And I believe that Georgina's faith in God is much stronger than mine, but she never boasts. She is a marvellous young woman indeed, and I have Sir Dominic to thank for bringing her so suddenly and so wonderfully into my life.

WEDNESDAY 16 APRIL 2014 (DAY 4)

Late at night, while Sir Dominic was asleep, I checked my e-mails and my Facebook. I was pleased to see an appreciative e-mail from Georgina, congratulating me on my helpful work with Sir Dominic. Coming from her, the congratulations touched my heart more than any other compliment. I returned the compliment and promised to keep her in touch with all developments.

Then I opened my Facebook page and got the shock of my life: there, in the middle of the page, was a post from Oscar with a big picture and a caption. The caption read: "Me and my sexy new girlfriend Sandy". The picture showed Oscar smiling with his usual, cheesy grin, with his arms around the shoulder of a tall, red-haired woman with intense green eyes. He was looking lustfully at her in the picture, but she was looking into the camera with an intense stare that gave me the creeps. The picture looked like it had been taken inside Oscar's flat, because the background was just a dull, off-white coloured wall.

But the woman in the picture was—Cassandra!

Naturally, I have never seen Cassandra, but by instinct I was sure that it was she. The nickname was further evidence. How could I not have realised that Sandy could be short for Cassandra? If Oscar had said "Cassie" or "Cass", I would have known straight away, but Cassandra is no fool, and would not have given herself away so easily. It all makes sense now: Oscar thought she was Dutch, and finds her hard to understand. Of course he would, if Cassandra speaks to him in Middle English!

I was now trembling. As Sir Dominic once said, Cassandra was a "lioness enraged in search of prey, prowling" through the streets in secret. But why did she go after Oscar? After some thought, I remembered that Oscar greeted Sir Dominic and me on Sunday afternoon. Cassandra must have seen him with us, followed him to the Fountain restaurant, and seduced him. And Oscar thinks that she is his new "girlfriend"? Oscar himself said that he can barely understand her, but he is only interested in one thing anyway. I mean, he could hardly remember her name the next day! But Cassandra wants far more. This reminds me of—

Tristan Miller!

I must go to see Oscar later today and warn him to leave Cassandra before it is too late. Perhaps he will come to his senses and flee for his life and soul, like Tristan.

I left Sir Dominic in my flat after breakfast and, under the pretext of running some errands, I went to Oscar's flat on

Regent Street. I felt bad concealing this from Sir Dominic, but after thinking about it, I decided that going alone was better, since Oscar was my friend, and I did not wish to embarrass him in front of a stranger.

I called Oscar on the way to make sure that he was alone.

When he let me in, he was still in his pyjamas, barefoot and unshaven, even though it was around eleven. He did not smell that good either.

But the state of his flat was unbelievable! What a dump! There were dishes and food waste all over the place! There were even some cockroaches and ants in the kitchen and living room.

"Oscar, what a pigsty! What have you done to this place?"

"Sorry, mate, I haven't had much time to clean up. Please make yourself at home."

"Oscar," I protested, "I am not a pig!"

"What are you saying, mate? That I am a pig? Are you judging me?"

"No, I'm judging this place! I know you; you may be a bit lazy and untidy, but you've never been as bad as this! Is it because you're too busy to keep a clean home?"

"Yeah, Sandy keeps me so busy. She is bloody insatiable!"

"Oscar, I beg you, leave her! Leave her at once! She's bad news!"

"Why, because you want her for yourself? No way, mate, she's mine! Anyway, I thought you liked blokes!"

I chose to ignore that stupid comment about my tendencies.

"Oscar, why are you still with her? Look what she's done to you! You're a filthy mess!"

"Hey, watch it mate! Look, she's my bird and she looks after me …"

His bird? More like his vulture!

"I don't understand her much," he continued, "she's a bit nuts, but I love that about her. She spends hours talking to herself in the mirror in some strange mumbo jumbo lingo, but I don't mind, because she's so sexy, and literally sets the bed on fire."

I was not sure how "literal" his description of their carnal affairs really was, but with the witch Cassandra, anything is possible.

"She is just so good in bed, mate! I really love to—"

He must have seen my expression of disgust (I knew what kind of lewd remark he was going to make), and so he changed his expression, saying with a mock posh accent, "Oh, I do apologise, Dr Arden! I mean to say that I greatly enjoy possessing her."

"I think that she's possessing you!"

"Hey mate, have you finished your sermon yet? Here, take a toffee apple and keep your gob shut!"

He offered me what looked like a toffee apple, a standard apple with a caramelised covering, but with no stick. I declined politely, and noticed that he took it from a bowl containing more of them, some of them half eaten.

"Sandy made these for me and for some other bird, her sister, I think."

Another girl? Did he mean Rose? If my suspicions were correct, Rose is alive somewhere! I breathed a sigh of relief. But I needed to see her for myself.

"May I use your toilet, Oscar?"

"Sure, it's over there, be my guest. I'm just going to put on some clothes, 'cause Sandy's coming back soon."

I froze in fear, but tried to conceal it in a mask of civility.

"That's all right. That will give me a chance to … meet her," I said, with a gulp.

While Oscar was in his room, I went to look around the flat. I looked in every room, even the toilet (which was really a sickening sight). I looked in every room that I could see, except Oscar's bedroom, but there was no sign of Rose anywhere.

Suddenly, Oscar came out and caught me snooping around.

"Are you right, mate?"

I tried to sneak a peek into his bedroom, but I did not have a chance to look closely. There was a click in the lock and the door knob turned. And in came Cassandra! Man, that idiot Oscar even gave her his key!

Cassandra seemed shocked at first, then she regained her composure. She turned to Oscar, grabbed his collar and lifted him off the ground.

"I see that you have brought a friend! Well done, knave!"

Yes, that was definitely Cassandra. That's how she talked to Tristan when she was displeased with him. If she only knew how well I knew her!

"Hey Sandy, don't get your knickers in a knot!"

It was clear that Oscar barely understood what she said, and she barely understood him. It was crystal clear that they were using clues from their body language to understand each other. I was trying to figure out if Cassandra's comment was sarcastic.

"Cassandra, where have you taken Rose Thorne?" I asked her point-blank.

I am not sure what shocked her more: my command of her Middle English dialect, my knowledge of her real name or my awareness of what happened to Rose. After her momentary surprise, she laughed.

"I see that you are a good friend of Sir Dominic!" she almost spat out his name in contempt. *"Very clever!"*

"So where is she? Where have you taken her?"

"I have not 'taken' her anywhere, knave!" protested Cassandra, feigning innocence.

"Liar! You use that mirror in your belt to disguise yourself as different people, then you try to abduct Rose and ruin her future marriage with her rightful betrothed, Sir Dominic!"

Cassandra's face turned crimson with rage.

"You know too much, knave! It is none of your damn business where Rose is! And tell your friend, that fellow who calls himself a knight, if he wants to see his beloved Rose alive again, he must meet me here tomorrow night, after midnight. Now go!"

With a shout and a clap of her hands, the front door flew open, and she pointed to the hallway. So, I thought, she has learnt a new magical trick! I left, noticing Oscar who was muttering to himself, "This is weird crap!" The door closed behind me and I ran all the way home. I stopped for breath outside my flat, called Georgina and asked her to come urgently to my place.

Sir Dominic was concerned when he saw me.

"Professor, why are you so pale and breathless? What ghost has petrified you to this point?"

I sat down, took my breath, drank a glass of water, and told Sir Dominic everything that happened in Oscar's flat. Soon after I had completed my narration to him, Georgina arrived, and I repeated it to her.

"You went to Oscar's flat when you knew that you might run into Cassandra?" she exclaimed. "Man, you have courage!"

"Indeed he has, and fortune favours the brave," said Sir Dominic.

"There is another reason to rejoice:
It seems so clear Cassandra has kept Rose
My darling is alive, although imprisoned.
Cassandra wishes that I go confront her.
I must then go and rescue Rose tomorrow
And wrest her from Cassandra's evil grasp.
This is my obligation as a knight
My honour and my name depend upon it.
If we are not united once again,
Before the clock strikes midnight of day six …"

Sir Dominic shuddered and then struck the table with his fist.

"No, failure cannot even be considered!
I promised Rose to give her my protection!
O Rose! My Rose! Dear God, protect my Rose!"

Sir Dominic wept.

It was moving and terrifying to see him weep. Georgina was also moved to tears and I wiped a few tears from my eyes too. Then we were all silent for a while, until I made a suggestion:

"Sir Dominic, why must we wait until midnight tomorrow? Why do we not call the police—the constables or soldiers who keep the

peace—storm Oscar's flat and take Rose away by force? That's much easier, is it not?"

Sir Dominic looked at me calmly before replying.

"If I, a knight, cannot deliver Rose
Without the aid of other knights, well then
I hardly do deserve the name of knight
And Rose will see a coward, not a man.
Cassandra, I am sure, is not a fool
She must have fed my darling with her lies
Seduced her to her side; she must have said
Sir Dominic her knight would never come
To rescue her and so she must be lost.
I go to face Cassandra on her terms
And free my Rose by faith and love alone."

"Gabriel," added Georgina, "from what I understood, Sir Dominic has to face Cassandra and rescue Rose by his love. Am I right?"

"Yes," I confirmed, "the magic mirror, which let him come here, said to him, 'True love alone will find the way.'"

Sir Dominic turned to me and said,

"Do mark this maiden, Gabriel, her mind
Is so astute, she is a jewel indeed!"

"I know," I said, full of warm feelings of affection mixed with admiration.

Georgina blushed.

She really is a wonderful, delightful, gorgeous young lady.

Sir Dominic became solemn again.

"Then so be it, my friends," said Sir Dominic, *"The sorceress Desires a confrontation, she shall have it!"*

THURSDAY 17 APRIL 2014 (DAY 5)

Sir Dominic and I went to the morning service at Great St Mary's Church today. He was deep in prayer, and I was deep in sleep, trying desperately to stay awake.

As I always say, I do believe in God, in my own way, but I have never attended a church service before today (except for some weddings and funerals), and I do not understand much about Christianity, except what I can glean from my mediaeval studies.

The sermon was long and monotonous, and all that I understood was that today is Maundy Thursday, commemorating Jesus Christ's Last Supper with his disciples before he was arrested and crucified.

After the service, Sir Dominic was silent until we exited the church and shook hands with Reverend Christopher. I dared not open my mouth or look either of the men in the eye, since I had slept through the sermon and I was quite embarrassed. But Sir Dominic had noticed it anyway. As we left, he said,

"I hope that you have had your fill of rest
For on this night, you must remain awake
Keep vigil, stay alert, I need support
From you and from Georgina when we go
To meet Cassandra at the flat tonight
Your spirit wills it, but your flesh is weak."

At seven o'clock, Georgina, her friend Veronica, Sir Dominic and I left my flat where we met earlier and went to a restaurant not far from the University. Sir Dominic was dressed in his mediaeval clothes again, including his sword, which he hid under a coat that I let him borrow. He carried a single rose in the inside pocket of the coat, which he probably intended to give to Rose.

When the waiter showed us to our table, we sat down to share our last meal together before Sir Dominic's confrontation with Cassandra. He was quiet and sad, as if he felt that he was going to die trying to rescue Rose.

We ate our meal in silence, only interrupted by banal conversation with the waiter who took our order. Sir Dominic ate nothing but some bread and a little wine.

During dinner, Sir Dominic held Georgina's hand and mine, (Georgina held Veronica's hand) and said,

"My friends, this meal shall be the last we share
Before I go my way to end my quest.
Whatever the result, I say farewell."

Georgina leaned over to translate for Veronica, but started to cry and found it hard to continue. Sir Dominic continued with quivering voice,

"But be of good cheer, this is why I came
To find my lovely Rose and set her free
And then return with her in victory
To life in fourteen hundred and fourteen.
When we are in the place of confrontation
I pray that you will stay close by my side
Supporting me in any way you can
Until I rescue Rose and take her back."

We all heartily expressed our feelings of loyalty and solidarity, even Veronica, who only partially understood the words but felt the emotions deeply.

At the end of the meal, at around 10:30, I paid the bill and we left the restaurant, making our way slowly towards Oscar's flat in Regent Street. Sir Dominic insisted that we all step into a chapel on the way to pray. Then, at around 11:30, we continued on our way towards the flat. Sir Dominic was silent, but tears were streaming down his face. Veronica took out a handkerchief and wiped his cheeks for him. Georgina also cried silently, and I gave her my handkerchief too.

At 11:55, we knocked on Oscar's door. He opened, surprised to see us all coming to meet him at this late hour. I reminded him (or explained, since he had little idea what was going on) that Cassandra was meeting us here with Rose.

"Oh, you're here for a party? That's cool! It's all good mate. Sandy, or Cassandra as you call her, is coming back here soon, I think. She went out with her sister, but she is coming soon. It's so hard to understand a bloody word she says, but if you say she's coming, she's coming. That's my girl, she always keeps her word."

Poor deluded Oscar! Only a miracle can save him now!

We sat down at the living room table of his squalid flat, waiting for Cassandra to make her appointment.

FRIDAY 18 APRIL (DAY 6)

It was at around a quarter past twelve this morning, while I was dozing off on Oscar's living room table, that Sir Dominic exclaimed,

"Behold she comes, but she is not alone!
Alas, how she has changed in form and raiment!"

I looked up as there came through the door a young woman with a blond crew-cut hairstyle, a leather jacket, shorts and black boots that reached high up to her shins. She was accompanied by another man, whom I could swear I had seen before, but could not remember from where. He was tall, had a crew-cut hairstyle too, with an earring and a beard. He too had a leather jacket and wore long jeans. Following them not far behind was Cassandra, in her own green kirtle and black shoes. This was a new strategy of Cassandra's, to come as herself!

How Sir Dominic recognised Rose in that young blonde woman was anyone's guess, but he knew Rose so well, no disguise was impenetrable, and magic was not involved here.

The young couple and Cassandra greeted Oscar, who fumbled about, trying to kiss Cassandra. Cassandra put her index finger to his lips, telling him to wait, and stood next to the door as Rose and the bearded man went to sit on the couch, walking past us and Sir Dominic as if we were not there. But Sir Dominic did not let this rudeness discourage him. As the strong, resolute knight that he was, intent on rescuing his damsel, Sir Dominic approached Rose who was reclining on the couch with her arm around the man, stood squarely in front of her, took out the rose that he had been carrying and presented it to her.

"My fairest Rose, I greet thee with this rose.
Thanks be to God, at last we are together!"

"Who are you?" asked Rose coldly.

I looked over at Cassandra, who was standing near the door, leaning against the wall with her arms crossed. She seemed pleased with herself and was grinning smugly.

"My Rose, 'tis I", continued Sir Dominic, *"thy future bridegroom, Dominic.*

Most certainly thou knowest who I am!"

"No, I know you not!" she replied coldly.

Cassandra Caligo cackled.

The bearded man started to kiss Rose's neck and she giggled like a little girl being tickled. He stared at Sir Dominic, as if to tell him with his eyes to give up and leave. Sir Dominic was visibly hurt by Rose's cold denial, but persevered.

"I came across the ages just to save thee
And take thee back with me to be my bride."

"I know you not, sir!" replied Rose again, in the same cold manner as before. *"And I assure you, I have no need to be saved."*

Cassandra Caligo cackled.

The tall bearded man rose to his feet like a clumsy bear being awoken from its slumber. He stood as tall as Sir Dominic and glowered at him.

"You heard her, mate! Leave the girl alone!"

Good heavens! He had the same accent as Oscar. I remembered his face now: it was one of Oscar's drinking buddies. What was his name again?

"It's all right, Bruce! Let him talk!"

I looked around in surprise at Cassandra. It was she who said those words, in the same modern East-End London accent as Oscar's! Oscar was standing next to her like a loyal puppy, but his eyes had a glazed-over look, as if his brain had been sucked out of his head. Was it possible that Cassandra had learned to speak like Oscar? She mimicked him perfectly. Yes, of course she could do that! She did it with Tristan, Sir Dominic, Rose's mother and many others, did she not?

Sir Dominic was deeply hurt, but not ready to give up on his betrothed, for whom he came six hundred years into the future.

"My sweetest Rose, what sorcery is this?
Who dares to steal thy memory of me?"

Sorcery? Of course! Cassandra was surely behind this! She must have used some sort of mind-altering drug on Rose (and probably on Oscar too), some potion or substance which either erased Rose's memory or brainwashed her. I remembered those apples in Oscar's kitchen, one of which he offered me a couple of days ago.

This was definitely Cassandra's cruellest trick, worse than murder or physical harm. With this trick, she did far worse than just kill Rose, she murdered the love and intimacy between Rose and Sir Dominic. Georgina and Veronica sat and watched in shock and disbelief, ready for anything.

Rose answered again,

"I know you not, sir. Pray trouble me no more."

Then she turned again to the bearded man, Bruce, who was sitting with her on the couch, put her arms around his neck and kissed him.

Cassandra Caligo cackled.

If this were not unnerving enough, she then started to taunt Sir Dominic.

"Behold the valiant, noble knight! His precious Rose has been plucked by another man! His Rose has been deflowered! Sir Dominic, prove your valour to us! Take out your sword and slay your rival! But Rose is lost to you forever!"

Her cackle resounded throughout the flat like a hyena about to devour its prey.

Sir Dominic did nothing. He bowed his head and prayed. He stood there, in front of his seemingly unfaithful fiancée and the bearded stranger, who were kissing and hugging in complete disregard for him, and prayed for about one minute. It was the longest minute of the night for us, who were his friends, and for Cassandra too, who stopped cackling and stared at him in disbelief. Sir Dominic then opened his eyes, knelt down in front of Rose, who noticed him now, and said these words:

"I promised to protect thee, as I could
And I should die before I let thee fall.
I came across six centuries to find thee
And though thou art transformed, I know thee well.
Let history record it in her pages,
I love thee with a love that spans the ages."

To Sir Dominic's delight and relief, a tear rolled down Rose's cheek. She looked at the rose that she had hastily and rudely discarded next to her on the couch, took it up again, smelt it, and started to cry.

She recognised him at last!

After that, everything happened very fast as the situation turned to chaos.

Cassandra pushed Oscar towards Sir Dominic, whispering the word "Go". Oscar went over to Sir Dominic, who was still kneeling and looking up at Rose, elated that Rose finally remembered him. Oscar tapped him on the shoulder and said, "Excuse me, mate."

Bruce, now enraged that Rose turned her attention away from him and was paying attention to Sir Dominic, rose to his feet and was about to attack him. But I came from behind him and wrapped my arm around his neck with a vice-like grip. Bruce struggled and grunted, but I had the element of surprise on my side, as well as the stronger position. Veronica came around in front of him with a knife and held it to his throat.

Cassandra flew in swiftly and struck Sir Dominic on the head from behind. He groaned and fell to the floor, bleeding from the crown of his head. Rose shouted his name and rushed to his side, kneeling down beside him. Georgina rushed over to Cassandra ready to punch her in the face, but Cassandra scratched her on the neck. Georgina screamed. Cassandra kicked Sir Dominic in the mouth and blood trickled from his lips. Georgina grabbed Cassandra from behind and held her arms in a vice-like grip. Oscar, looking around like a deer in headlights, was at a complete loss what to do.

In all the commotion, I saw Sir Dominic as he raised himself painfully off the floor, looked up at Rose and tried to speak, but he was bleeding from the mouth. Rose held his head in her arms and cried inconsolably.

"O Dominic, forgive me!"

Sir Dominic, with all the strength that he could muster, said to her in a soft, gentle voice,

"O Rose, thy mind was captive, held in check
But now thou art released, my dearest dove.
No person on this earth can ever wreck
Our deep and everlasting, boundless love."

Cassandra struggled to free herself from Georgina's grip but felt the cold point of a knife in her back. It was Oscar holding the knife! He too must have been released from his zombie-like trance, and finally realised what was going on. He must have finally realised that Cassandra had used him callously to plan this malicious trick on Sir Dominic. He must have awoken to his senses and decided now to do the right thing. Good old Oscar! He might be crude at times, he might have lost his mind, but his heart is in the right place.

Cassandra saw him out of the corner of her eye and screamed, "ET TU, OSCAR?" ("And you too, Oscar?").

Sir Dominic raised himself again, wincing in pain and with blood-stained face and lips, and kissed Rose gently on her lips.

"Now it is … finished."

With those final words, he fell to the floor, lifeless.

I heard a clap of thunder outside, and then the sound of heavy rain.

Then there was an almighty banging on the door. We heard a shout from outside. "Open up! This is the police! Open up, or we'll break the door down!"

One of the neighbours must have called 999, the emergency number, because of all the screaming and the violence taking place next door.

Rose, looking at her knight, her betrothed, her hero, lying lifeless with his sorely wounded head in her lap, started to cry out to him,

"I love thee!

I love thee!

I love thee!"

There was a sound of glass cracking. Cassandra's hand-held mirror, which was hanging from her belt, fell to the floor. There was a large, ugly crack in it from top to bottom. Then, almost instantaneously, all the other mirrors in the flat cracked from top to bottom as well! Oscar and Bruce looked around in shock, muttering, "What the … !"

Cassandra Caligo cursed and cried out. I followed her gaze and beckoned to Georgina and Veronica. They looked too, then looked up to heaven and exclaimed, "Thanks be to God! True love alone did find the way!"

Sir Dominic and Rose had disappeared! There was not a single trace of them there! The spell which brought them here was broken!

Georgina answered the violent knocks on the door and opened for the police. They quickly surveyed the scene and seized Cassandra, handcuffed her and Bruce, and led them away. Cassandra was cursing in Latin and Middle English. Georgina, Veronica and I followed the police to the station.

The time on the clock was five minutes to one.

"V for Victory", said Georgina to me.

That was the shape that the two hands of the clock were making.

The police were baffled by Cassandra Caligo: she had no identification papers, and could not speak any contemporary English. They called me and inquired about her language and background, since I was a language professor. I told them that she was an intelligent student who went mad, and this was true in a way, according to Brother Benedict. Because of her lack of papers, she was locked in detention as an illegal immigrant. Bruce was released with no charges.

I chose not to give the police my tape recording. How could it have helped them anyway? It would have just created more problems too difficult to explain. I have decided not to let anyone listen to this recording, except Georgina.

Oscar apologised profusely for what he had done, and we forgave him. He is now undergoing extensive psychotherapy. Bruce, his friend, joined him. He just does not know what to make of the whole experience.

Georgina recovered in hospital (I took her there), because none of her wounds was life-threatening. I sat by her bedside and we talked about the great events of this past week.

"Thanks be to God," said Georgina, "Sir Dominic and Rose went back to their time."

"How can you be so sure?" I asked.

"O Doubting Thomas, look at the evidence! They disappeared completely when Cassandra's spell was broken. Her mirror fell and cracked from top to bottom. She screamed and cursed, and when your enemy does that, you know that she is defeated. Sir Dominic won Rose's heart within the period stipulated by the magic mirror in 1414. He conquered hate and evil with true love, which sacrifices everything for the beloved."

"That's true, but I need to see more evidence that he made it back safely."

"You will, in time. But consider this: in your paper on the *Confessions of Brother Benedict*, you say that Tristan makes it clear that no one ever heard from Cassandra again, and that her house was vacant. That is because she is stuck here, in detention, and will probably never make it back. But Brother Benedict never talks about the disappearance of Sir Dominic and Rose, as far as we know. Why do you think that is?"

"Of course! Because they returned safely to their time, at exactly the time that they left. Or the time that Sir Dominic left. It was as if nothing had ever happened!"

"As if nothing had ever happened, exactly! And because the spell was broken, I believe that Sir Dominic's deadly injuries disappeared."

"I am not a hundred percent certain about that, Georgina. I hope so, but I suppose that we shall never really know. I am certain that if he returned with those injuries, he would have been healed in his own time. We shall probably never know how Rose appeared when she returned to her time. Did she reappear with her crew-cut hairstyle and strange, modern clothing? Anyway, these are minor details, and they preserve the mystery surrounding these spectacular events."

"Remember, Gabriel, that they entered our time through a mirror in a dress shop. When they returned, they could easily have changed Rose's clothes before she returned to her home."

"Yes, that's true."

"And Rose's mother and father, who saw Sir Dominic enter the mirror, would have seen him come back with Rose almost immediately afterwards, in a matter of seconds, or minutes. Who knows?"

"And who cares? I don't think that Rose's parents would go telling anyone about that. They would be thanking God for the miracle and trying to forget the whole sordid affair of Cassandra's treacherous envy."

I looked at Georgina and smiled. Georgina is the most beautiful, most intelligent young lady that I have ever known. I am now irrevocably, irresistibly and irrefutably in love with her.

"Georgina, I am sorry that you were injured in the fray. I wish that I could have prevented that."

"No, don't worry about it. Thank God that it was not worse, and that Sir Dominic was victorious in his quest."

Then what she said next surprised me so much that I had trouble keeping my mouth closed.

"Thank God for Dominic, thank God for Rose,
Thank God, that by His providence He chose
Both thee and me to aid them in the quest,
Thereby our lives have been forever blessed.
For thee I have the deepest admiration
Not just for thy great knowledge and high station
But more for thy great valour and thy heart
So full of selfless love in every part.
For this, my dearest man, thou art to me
My hero, I would die to be with thee."

I had tears streaming down my cheeks. I was at a loss for words, which is rare for me as a professor. After sobbing with deep joy and deep emotion, and hugging Georgina warmly, I found the words with which to reply.

"In debt to thee I shall forever be
Without thy priceless aid, o how could we
Have found the maiden Rose and rescued her?
Although I lacked the courage, I aver,
To call thee months ago, it was decreed
By destiny that thou and I did need
To be together, dear Georgina fair.
For this, with borrowed words, I do declare,
In every day of life, through all its stages
I love thee with a love that spans the ages."

END OF PART 2

~Part 3~

The End and the Beginning

SUNDAY 20 APRIL 2014

Georgina was discharged from hospital on Friday night. Yesterday, she and I attended the evening paschal mass together. I went merely for solidarity to Georgina, and in honour of Sir Dominic, who in many ways has become a real friend to me, even though he now lives six hundred years before me.

It was then, in Great St Mary's Church, that a miracle occurred, which I find it hard to explain. As I was sitting in the pew next to Georgina, I understood what Reverend Christopher said in the sermon, and I understood the whole meaning of the service for the first time in my life. It all started to make sense to me.

I was thinking of Sir Dominic and Rose, and all the spectacular events that have taken place in their lives and ours, in 1414 and over the last week in 2014. I thought especially about Sir Dominic's words and private deeds, like his prayers, which defused Cassandra's spells. I remembered Cassandra's evil ways, and as I shuddered, I thanked God that her wicked deeds were now just a horrible nightmare that has faded in the morning light. I thought about poor Rose Thorne, who suffered so much at the envious Cassandra's hands, and about Sir Dominic's deep love for Rose, a love so strong that he came to our time to save her. Strangely enough, the reverend also gave a sermon about the same kind of love.

Today, Easter Sunday, Georgina and I attended the Easter service in the morning, and afterwards, we shook hands with Reverend Christopher on the way out.

"Happy Easter, Dr Arden and Miss Olivet. Dr Arden, it's great to see you awake this time!"

I laughed, and replied, "I am a different man, Reverend. And it's all thanks to a dear friend of mine."

"You mean the knight who was with you on Maundy Thursday? The same man who came here with you, looking for a young blonde woman on Palm Sunday?"

"Yes, that's right!" I exclaimed in surprise. "You have a good memory, Reverend! But how did you know that he was a knight? I introduced him as a friend."

"I shall tell you later. Dr Arden, Miss Olivet, please see me in half an hour in the rectory. I have something very important to show you."

Georgina and I could hardly wait. What he wanted to show us was probably related to Sir Dominic and Rose, but what? That half hour could not have passed quickly enough!

Reverend Christopher took us to the rectory and closed the door.

"Friends, what I am about to show you is remarkable, and will certainly bring you good cheer. Remember, I believe in miracles too, and this is an incredible miracle. I do not know how Sir Dominic and Rose came to our time, but it certainly happened. The Lord moves in mysterious ways! Anyway, as I was saying, after Dr Arden came with his friend, who was dressed as a knight, on Palm Sunday, I thought at first that he was an actor, or just in fancy dress. But the name Dominic Wright rang a bell. But it was only when Dr Arden came with Sir Dominic on Thursday, and I heard Sir Dominic speak to him in perfect Middle English, that my suspicions were confirmed. This was no ordinary man! I am familiar with some mediaeval history and literature too, Dr Arden! I started to do some research of my own into the church archives. After extensive study of all the church archives in Cambridgeshire, I found this."

Reverend Christopher presented us with a document, which was a bit old and worn, but still legible.

"Dr Arden, would you do the honours?"

I read the document carefully. It was a record of Sir Dominic's and Rose Lady Wright's death and burial, recorded on 4 August 1443.

"They died on the same day!" exclaimed Georgina.

"Sir Dominic was born on 4 August 1393, which was St Dominic's day", I continued. "His wife, Rose, died on 4 August 1443, at the ripe old age (by mediaeval standards) of forty-seven. Sir Dominic, unable to live without his beloved, died shortly afterwards, on the same day. Rose Lady Wright gave him seven children, whose names were …"

I froze, then trembled. I dropped the document, then picked it up again to continue reading.

"... whose names were Gabriel, Georgina, Veronica
..."

"Is it possible," asked Georgina, trembling in turn, "that they named their first children after us?"

"Yes, in fact, that is what they did," I answered. "Listen to this epitaph in verse, which is also found on Sir Dominic's tombstone in Ely Cathedral. I shall translate it for you into Modern English:

"Dear friends, my wife and I together greet you
And wish you well, and thank you for your pains.
God bless you both and grant you every joy
Your aid was indispensable to us,
And we were married all because of you.
In spite of the great distance which divides us
We feel that you are ever present here.
You will be pleased to know that we have named
Our first three children after all of you.
Pray know that you are always in our prayers
For you are in the hands of Him who holds
All ages from the first until the last."

Georgina, Reverend Christopher and I stood in awe for at least two minutes, trying to absorb the magnitude of this discovery. Not only did Sir Dominic and Rose go back to their time, but they had a long and happy life together (by mediaeval standards anyway), and Rose gave her knight seven healthy children, three of whom bore our names. And finally, they loved each other so much that they passed away and went to the Lord together.

Tonight, I took Georgina to dinner in the same restaurant in which Sir Dominic shared his last meal with us. After I escorted her home, I sat down in my bed and read the Gospel, and for the first time, I understood it properly. I knew parts of it before, indirectly through literature, but not from beginning to end, and in detail. After reading the marvellous story of Jesus Christ, I got under the covers and fell asleep. And while I was asleep, I had an unusual dream.

I was in a large banquet hall, far more spacious, far more sumptuous and far more splendid than any mediaeval manor house. It was a bright, sunny day, and the sun's rays were streaming through the open windows, bathing everything in dazzling light. There were hundreds of people present, all dressed in white, some of them sounding golden trumpets.

Then I beheld the Bride as she entered the hall and made her way towards the front of the hall, where her Bridegroom awaited her. She had crystalline blue eyes and long, golden hair, all pulled up and braided; she was dressed in a long, white wedding dress, whiter than snow, with a long train. She wore a shining silver tiara, decorated with red roses all around its base. She also carried a large bouquet of red, white, pink and yellow roses. She was smiling, and she had tears in her eyes for sheer joy. As she made her way towards the Bridegroom, everyone stood and cheered.

She finally reached her Bridegroom, who was smiling at her in uncontainable bliss. He took her hand in his and sang this song to her:

"My love, thou art the dearest rose of all
Thou art my chosen flower, thee I call
My pride, my beauty, source of my delight
The most adored and precious in my sight.
No one can ever snatch thee from my hand
I shall protect thee always, and shall stand

Beside thee, watching thee and loving thee
Eternally shalt thou abide with me.
Beyond this age my love for thee extends
I love thee with a love that never ends."

The Bride seemed to glow with a brighter hue as the Bridegroom sang these words to her. I beheld the Bride more closely. In her bouquet, which contained roses of different colours, I saw myself within the rose petals. I also saw Georgina, Veronica, my family, my friends—even Oscar and Bruce. Then I saw all of the people of England and the world—past, present and future.

I beheld the Bridegroom, who was also dressed in white, with a garment so white, no launderer on earth could have made it whiter. As I gazed into His kind, gentle and beautiful face, I saw a love like no other, a love that radiated from His eyes and smile and reached into my soul. I felt that He was speaking to me when He repeated these words,

"Beyond this age, my love for thee extends
I love thee with a love that never ends."

I awoke with tears streaming down my cheeks. I arose from my bed, knelt down on the floor beside it, and bowed my head to the wonderful Bridegroom in my dream, whom I recognised as Jesus Christ. He is the valiant Knight and Bridegroom, and Humanity is the Bride, whom He rescued from the claws of evil by His Love—a Love that spans the ages, a Love that never ends.

I answered Him with the words that I learnt from Rose Thorne, and which now flowed naturally to my lips,

"I love Thee,

I love Thee,

I love Thee!"

This may seem to be the end of my story, but really, it is also the beginning of a new story.

ABOUT THE AUTHOR

Emile N. Joseph is of Egyptian origin and was raised in a Christian family. He attended an Anglican School and graduated with Honours from the University of Sydney. Since 2000, he has been teaching English in an adult migrant college.

Joseph is happily married with two children and lives in Sydney, Australia. He is passionate about all aspects of language, especially its history, and is fluent in English, French and Italian.

www.ingramcontent.com/pod-product-compliance
Lightning Source LLC
Chambersburg PA
CBHW020146180626
46810CB00004B/1761